FANTASTIC WRITERS AND WHERE TO READ THEM

FANTASTIC WRITERS

Creative Hats

First published in Great Britain, 2022 by C H Press, a division of Creative Hats.

First published in hardback in Hertfordshire in 2022 by C H Books, an imprint of Creative Hats.

This paperback edition published in 2022.

Cover design by: C H Books

Edited by: Lewis Green

FANTASTIC WRITERS &
WHERE TO READ THEM

Fantastic Contributors:

Bob Bootman

Lewis Green

Martyn Kempson

Nicola Warner

Paul Clark

Tina Cooper

Tricia Ramsay

CONTENTS

vi

Foreword
by Kelly Hatley

Bob, Lewis, Martyn, Nicola, Paul, Tina, and Tricia met while studying creative writing at their local college. I had the pleasure of being their teacher – though I'm sure I learn just as much from them week on week.

This collection of creative work is a result of their ongoing commitment to the craft. They are 'fantastic' and they are 'writers' maybe not ... J K Rowling epic yet - but give them time!

Speaking of Rowling – and just for additional legal clarity - this book has no connection whatsoever to any franchise associated with her or her collection of work. Breathe. The book title was a tongue-in-cheek suggestion from her super fan Nicola and I felt it had a feel-good flavour to it. So it evolved and stuck.

Afterall, how often do creative writers hide behind imposter fears and worry about even calling themselves, 'writers'. This is very much a book to inspire. Each member sends their collective expression of, 'if we can do it - so can you!'

pp. 8-23

Okay introductions complete – what's in here? Aside from 'fantastic writers' . Well, the book opens with **A to Z** poems. Why not have a go? Or if you fancy a bonus you could watch some behind the scenes footage of Bob and Martyn playing ping pong poetry during class – www.creativehats.co.uk/fantasticwriters

pp. 26-32

Backchat is a section dedicated to talking back to other creative work, a societal issue, or tutor - as was the case with Kia Aura when Bob decided to mock my love of Kia Carens' after a huge amount of work was fixed within warranty! Read it in good spirits – no lawsuits please and thanks.

pp. 54-63

Skipping to **Extracts**, here you can sample prose from upcoming novels.

pp. 110-115

Inspirational, like other categories could have housed heaps but opted for pieces about writing and anything which prompted new work. Go on, get out that notepad and write.

pp. 148-150

Love opens with a dying plant, photographed in Mrs Howard's Memorial Hall, where the groups meet. I joked with Bobby the manager, that I hadn't prepared a creative exercise that week and leaving the plant may inspire some work. It did – even if in jest.

pp. 184-185 & 260-266

Obtuse was a section along with **War Poetry** which yielded much debate about what and who can write certain pieces of work. The group were encouraged to 'try' and never be afraid to tackle anything if they had the reasoning to want to.

pp. 200-205

Reflections had to be given to our queen of creative non-fiction and life writing - Tina Cooper. Who managed to produce some excellent *fiction* of late – yet still protests any such talent in public. She had concerns about her piece, *The Dinner Party* on page x in case the reader wonders (not wanders ☺) why it is all in speech and felt a bit random. The brief *was* to write only in speech and include a well-known character from real life. Random!

pp. 304-308

Yikes! Had a similar origin which may benefit from an explanation. During Crime Week, the group played the paper kids party game where you come up with a character, flip over then pass to the next person, and keep adding to the story. Nicola and Bob were brave enough to turn their random illegible group notes into story gems.

pp. 268-298

A final mention to the **Xmas** section and nod to the fact that though we are releasing this book in Spring 2022, we will of course be reminding the world to buy this as Christmas gifts for friends and family each year! The gift that keeps on giving!

Be sure to check out each Author's acknowledgement at the end – and keep one ear to the ground for more books coming soon!

Thanks from Creative Hats to North Herts College, Mrs Howard's Memorial Hall, EIT Room, Chums Charity for all their support and being Creative Hat's recognised charity for the fantastic work they carry out, Gemma who went and had a baby rather than appear here - no excuses next time and of course the Fantastic Writers – Bob, Lewis, Martyn, Nicola, Paul, Tina and Tricia – Fantastic people – you deserve every success!

Final thanks to you, the reader who popped inside for a peek then stayed for the book! Please share the love with reviews, sales, social media and chocolate biscuits!

Until next time …

A to Z

Alice in Wonderland
by Bob Bootman & Martyn Kempson

Adventures await down a hole with a rabbit
Alice grasped for a key, but just couldn't grab it

By feeling and touching she found a small table
Bedecked with a tablet and bottle with label

Curious of mind she reads the instruction
Clueless the contents will cause size reduction

'Drink Me' it read and she gulped down a double
Drunk and stroppy and looking for trouble

Expeditiously shrinking she grabbed at the cake
'Eat Me' it said and a bite she did take

Furiously waving the fan made her shrink
Feet slipped down and she fell in the drink

Greeting a mouse, or was it a rat?
Gallically gargling "Ou est ma chatte?"

Hark ! Mr Dodo, I will be succinct
History tells me, you should be extinct

Inspired by the Dodo they're running a race
In a small circle at blistering pace

Jumps into the house in search for gloves
Just finds more juice, which we know she loves

Knows the consequence of taking a swig
Keeps gulping the liquid and starts to grow big

Lots of animals throwing debris
Lizard Bill climbs down the chimney

Magic mushrooms abound, caterpillar atop
Might take a bite, she just cannot stop

Now Masterchef final, it surely ain't
No croutons and soup as thick as paint

Observed cats without a grin like that
Oh! But never a grin without a cat!

Party time for all the lot
Poor dormouse placed inside the pot

Quick to the garden, roses previously red
Queenie is shouting, "OFF WITH HIS HEAD!"

Rescuing the Duchess from inside the 'nick'
Royal Highness is receiving some stick

Sad, even though he has no sorrow
Story of the Turtle won't wait 'til tomorrow

Turtle and Gryphon begin their prancing
Trying out moves for Strictly Come Dancing

Under the lights, Alice feels she's in heaven
"Underwhelming" says Craig, while Len gives a
"SEVEN"

Virginal Alice knocks the box of the jury
Volcanic rage adds to the Queen's fury

Witnesses called for the stealing of tarts
Witless judgements from the Queen of Hearts

"X-ecute, x-ecute, chop off her head!"
X-tremely wishing that Alice were dead

Yelling at Alice, "You're guilty as charged!"
"You must be gone, as you are enlarged!"

Zero story left to unroll, Alice lies on the grassy knoll

Zenith of our tale is finally over, now Alice rests upon the clover

Cinderella A to Z

by Martyn Kempson & Bob Bootman

A tale of a girl with a wicked step-mother

   Two awful sisters, without a brother

Bed was the floor of the cold attic room

   Asleep on the floor with her rags and a broom

Cinderella her name, as she sat by the fireplace

   Sisters quite jealous of her beautiful face

Demonstrably scared of her horrid step-mum

   But in case she got beaten, she wisely kept schtum

Everyone invited to the Prince's Ball

   Except Cinderella, that was the house rule

Frills and fripperies sewn on sister's dresses

Bows and ribbons tied on their tresses

Got them both ready and sprayed them with scent

Cinders waved them goodbye and cried when they went

Help was on hand to help the young lass

Now Cinderella was cooking with gas

In a flash a fairy godmother appeared

Armed with a pumpkin, which was a bit weird

"Jolly good, a pumpkin?" cried the girl

"My head has been turned, I'm in a whirl"

Knew that there was no time to waste

Transformed Cinderella, then they made haste

Lizards were caught and changed into staff

It was enough to make a cat laugh

Mice became horses in no time at all

Jumped into the coach and off to the ball

Now the Prince saw her dressed in sequins and gay

They waltzed all night as he swept her away

On the stroke of midnight he went for a grab

Cinderella was shocked, jumped into a cab

Prince discovered he fancied her lots

For the dancing girl he had the hots

Quickly got home, didn't know what to do

In the rush to get out, she lost her left shoe

"Rest assured," said the Prince, "I will not tarry"

"Whomsoever the shoe fits, I will marry"

Stepsisters stepped up and tried on the shoe

They were size ten, it was nearer size two

'T'was Cinders turn to try on the shoe

Fitted like a glove, as all could view

Understandably shocked, she started to wince

With her head held high, she rejected the Prince

Various thoughts ran through her mind

But thought she would stick with womankind

Was fairly certain she'd like to abscond

With the pumpkin girl and her magic wand

X-citedly made her love proposition

To the sorcerous, cute, wand-wielding magician

"Yes!" She cried, with tears of laughter

And so they lived happily ever after

"Zikes!" Howled the Prince, the dishonorable fella

He shouldn't have messed with Cinderella

Magic Roundabout

New soundtrack found by Paul Clark

Zebedee springs into view

Yes, early up with things to do

"Xcellent" he exclaims

Writing down his daily aims

Vehemently, Dougal appears

Under a cloud, too many beers

Telling all he's still a pup

Smarting from an Uber Sup!

Rolling her eyes Flo walks in

Questioning Dougal about where he's been

"Partridge and Dog" to start

Over the road to the, "Royal Hart".

Nearly reached, The Plough

Met Dylan, furloughed for now

Linked up with Brian the snail

Knew he'd be there for an ale

Joined Ermintrude for a chat

In the meadow with THAT hat!

Has anyone got ideas for today?

Growled Flo - in that *funny* way

Follow me we'll have a ramble

Ermintrude mooed, "I'd rather amble"

Dylan woke from his nap

Come on said Flo, I've got an App

Be back soon Zebedee said

And very soon, it's time for bed!

Snow White

by Paul Clark

A clearing silent in a wood

Belonging to a lady good

Cheery laughter always there

Delicious bites for all to share

Everyone welcome in this home

Fawns and rabbits and a little gnome

Greeting travelers from many miles

Hospitality and many smiles

Indigo through violet and red

Joyful with songs and bread

Kneading and singing every day

Loving all in every way

Monday they are dressed in yellows

Nodding to the beat those seven fellows

Opening the concert daily

Piping brings them out gaily

Queen rule is what they sing

Rattling their silver bling

Snow white is trilling, so listen

Tell all to come and listen

Underneath the forest leaves

Vaulting with flouncy sleeves

Welcome to short and tall

Xpect a glassful in the hall

You must come every year

Zenith to the end, the nadir!

Trouble in Toytown

by Paul Clark

A man called Noddy woke up with a sigh

Because he'd been caught by speeding eye

Constable Plod was away for the day

Detective Duck: he could make hay

Everyone knew about this sin

From Big Ears to Zippy Din

Glowering behind curtains shut

Hearing curses against him cut

Incurring laughter from Larry Lamb

Jarring phrases from Farmer Ham

Knowing Big Ears will come to aid

Lots of cash needed or a flashing blade

Matters to discuss a choice to make

Non-violence or more laws to break

Opportunities to be well wished

Police detective could be vanished!

Question is how to do the deed

Realization of detectives' greed

Saving on a need for speed

Time to make that damn Duck bleed

Under cover of darkness, they would go

Vengeance, be mine, Noddy says go!

When they got to the station

Xanthe explained Ducks on vacation

You can't be serious about your bill

You've been caught, it's first of April!

Woodland Freedom

by Paul Clark

After the crusades an archer returns

Back in the hood a tale he learns

Coming back with the Moor

Dastardly Sheriff bullies the poor

Events spiral to be the forest don

Fighting in river, Robin and Little John

Guy Gisbourne, the sheriff hench

Hurting villagers, fists clenched

Into the woods for food and drink

Jumping out for merchants' clink

Knaves, my gold, the Sherriff shrieks

Little John and Co, safe for weeks

Marion and Friar Tuck are on song

Now the plot all goes wrong

Oh Scarlet he turns his coat

Plot revealed, action rewrote

Quitting not a choice

Robin, a persuasive voice

Stopping the marriage match

There's plans to make a plot to hatch

Under cover is the key

Victory for all to see

When Richard the King appears

Xcitement galore, so many tears

Years of terror at an end

Zealous party hope to send.

Backchat

Homeless Britain Has Talent

by Martyn Kempson

On one leg, a booted stork,

the other straight, an arabesque

topped off with magazine in hand.

He has his act, his show, his costume perfected.

Homeless Britain has talent.

The lunchtime crowd use him

as a roundabout, a straining Eros,

steering left and right around him

avoiding the crash of eye contact.

He seems unperturbed, silent,

his story untold and Big Issue unsold.

Kia Aura

by Bob Bootman

Bought a brand-new Kia

1st June 2014

An automatic Sportage

Coloured luminescent green

One of the main attractions

Was a seven-year warranty

All mechanical faults would be rectified

Absolutely no cost to me

For seven years I loved that car

Drove it nearly every day

Confident that, if it went wrong

I wouldn't have to pay

Its performance was almost perfect

Sailed through every MOT

It purred just like a kitten

As it took me from A to B

***

On 2nd June 2021

My Kia wouldn't start

I opened up the bonnet

The engine blown apart

The warranty had ended

Repairs would cost the earth

Was quoted four and a half thousand pounds

Which was more than the car was worth

Collected by the breakers yard

Got one hundred quid for scrap

Never buy a brand-new Kia

They're a fucking pile of crap....

Still Life

by Lewis Green

The pile of bones still lay in the courtyard. For the second time that day the maid, laden with linen, passed the pile, which she swears has grown since this morning. It had been darker then, so she could have been mistaken. She was certain though, that the dried rind of oranges was a more recent addition. The oily sheen from the bones was now attracting the attention of the neighbourhood cats, which hiss and purr in chorus. She shoos the cats away with her foot and curses under her breath the person who left these scraps. *Probably that strange man on the third floor or the tramp on the corner*, she thinks. She heads back inside with the linen and has a coffee with the concierge before carrying on her rounds.

Across the city, a man sits alone at a table in Le Tambourin. He stares longingly at the owner and pours the last of the wine from a small carafe. He swallows it in one and heads for the door of the café. Tomorrow he shall return and do the same, he thinks. He must head to Les Halles before returning home. He needs another day with the fish – he hasn't got the light quite right yet. It shouldn't take much longer, he thinks. Theo is beginning to complain about the smell. He'll pick up another bag of oranges whilst he is here. He'll go the long way home as he likes to walk a while through the Tuileries. Tomorrow he shall do the same, he thinks.

Almost home, Rue Lepic. He must be careful to avoid that surly maid. She's always eyeing him suspiciously. Upstairs, he takes his time to set the table just right. The curtain has been tied the same way all week. He has kept it tied, even at night, to ensure the light on the table falls in the exact same place. *One more day*, he thinks, *then I can shut the curtains and get a good night's sleep. How those streetlamps keep me awake at night.*

He squints and walks around the table several times before sitting down to start his day's work. He chooses a clean brush and pushes it through the smudge of titanium white on the palette on his lap. He holds his breath as he adds tints of white to the canvas. He can hear the squabbling of cats outside the window. He scratches his beard and squints again at the canvas. He clenches and unclenches his fist, before wiping the brush on a rag dipped in turpentine. He is excited to show Theo when he returns from work. He walks to the window, opens it, and throws out the fish. When Theo gets home, they will share the oranges. He pulls the curtain to and lies down on the bed. Soon he will close his eyes and fall asleep. He will be awakened by the sound of the maid crossing the courtyard below his window. The sound of cats mewling. Paris coming to life.

Still Life with mackerel, lemon and tomato

Vincent Van Gogh, Paris, Summer 1886

***

To : William Carlos Williams

by Bob Bootman

This is Just to Say

I have read

Your poem

about plums

which

really annoyed me

as I ate

my breakfast

forgive me

it was rubbish

but not as bad

as your one about

the red wheelbarrow

PS even your name is a bit annoying

Comedy

To: Bob Bootman

by Tina Cooper

There once was a man with two plums

That were bigger than his massive thumbs

They were the colour maroon

But he admired them too soon

As they reduced and became rather humdrum

Trouble at the Palace

by Martyn Kempson

Six hundred for tea and the boiler's broke.

Charles declares it's beyond a joke.

The PM's coming with Sam Cam

and all one has is a tin of Spam.

The leckie's off and the plumber's out

The palace vibrates to Liz's shout

One'll fix it Charles, I'm not deterred

Because one is corgi registered!

Tuesday

by Bob Bootman

My brother is called Tuesday

Which is hard to be believed

My parents named him after the day

Not the place, he was conceived

How the hell did they remember that?

Why were they so precise?

You only have sex on a Tuesday

To celebrate something nice

He was born upon the 10th June

In 1965

During the swinging sixties

2 years before I was alive

9 months back, on a Tuesday

September, 64

My Dad had been away for a month

When he walked through the front door

It was my mother's birthday

He'd bought some lovely flowers

Apparently, she was very pleased

And they went upstairs

For hours...

They named him after that memorable day

Was bullied each day at school

It was irresponsible and mean

He was treated like a fool

If you feel sorry for my brother

With him, they laid down the mark

I was named after the place of my conception….

Hertford municipal car park

Bob Bootman (formerly Hertford municipal car park)

Sellotape a banana here

Death

Being Death's Messenger

by Tina Cooper

To be honest, it gets boring. After a few millennia of carrying out Death's work, because she's too damn lazy, the novelty has worn a little thin. Perhaps lazy is a tad harsh, there is much to do so delegating is the only sensible thing for it, but she doesn't collect anyone these days. I'm still in the dark as to why? Death just sits on her ridiculous, oversized, throne and watches us.

I say "throne" but it's more just a big chair, it's just bigger than all the other chairs.

When Death first mentioned the promotion, I couldn't believe my luck. Of course, I had always hoped to be noticed, I was meticulous when it came to the daily calculations and I took extra care before notifying my messenger. Not one single mistake in all those years yet others had been promoted before me, even Vector who sent his messenger to collect Billy Connolly. Thankfully word reached the messenger before he took Billy too soon, nobody wants to be known for that. Sending a messenger to collect the wrong soul would mean another getting more time than they were allocated which, as you know, would screw up all the timelines connected to that soul. It would be a disaster of catastrophic proportions. Mind you, it would be interesting to see… so long as it wasn't my mistake that caused it.

To my knowledge there has been only one early collection, just by a few minutes.

A last request went unsaid but it was ok, I don't think Hardy wanted to kiss him, so all was well that ended rather too quickly.

Anyway, I've strayed from the point.

I liked to think my staying put was because I was so good in my role that she didn't dare lose me, but I think it had more to do with the others just being louder. I wasn't one to brag, despite having good reason to do so, I worked quietly and efficiently. I worked unnoticed.

Or so I thought.

"I think you're ready," Death had said. "Something simple to begin with, an old man who is ready to come home. All you need to do is be there to point him in the right direction, he can manage the rest"

I thanked her too much, handed my death date calculator to the newbie, and left before Death could change her mind.

The old man was lovely, Death had been right, he was ready. I'd go so far as to say keen.

We chatted on the journey home, and he'd had a happy, productive, life but he'd lost his husband a few years before and hadn't coped very well. It was his time. The old man thanked me. I was thrilled, I felt as though I was in the right place, finally.

Many years have passed since then. So many souls I have collected and guided on their journeys home. The children are the hardest. Although they are never upset, souls tend not to be, I would chance a glimpse of their families before we left, and it never failed to stop me in my tracks. On one occasion it was a six-year-old girl who reminded me why we were there.

"Come on," she'd said, "let's go, my nanny is waiting."

I was lucky, she wasn't cross, and, to my knowledge, never told Death about it. Messengers are chosen for their kindness, for obvious reasons, but also for their unfaltering work ethic. Mine had faltered. I have been resolute ever since. There have been times where I have taken a quick sneaky peek at those left behind but I'm better at hiding it now. I know, it's wrong, I'm not supposed to, but it gives me a hint as to how much the soul was/is loved. In a strange way I like to know they'll be missed. I'll never be missed as I can't die but I like to imagine someone being sad that I've gone.

All was well in my world and heaven was, as always, a place where I felt at peace. I was happy.

There are many messengers, so we sometimes give each other a day off here and there. I love a day off; I will usually spend it visiting my souls to see how they are getting on. Of course, they are always doing well, some have even begun their work in the calculation's office, and some have gone on to become messengers themselves. Some had chosen to stay in heaven, with their loved ones, which was always lovely to see.

So why am I so despondent?

I had been sent to collect a man of the street. I had been warned that he was a loner, there was no family although there must have been at some point. I wondered where they were. Had they died before him, or had they left him? If so, why? Sadly, I'm not allowed to ask. I'm allowed to listen should any soul feel the need to talk but I can't offer an opinion or even nod in agreement. I just listen and guide them home.

I'm not sure what happened on the way down to earth, all I can tell you is that I felt different. Because of the way we travel we cannot be disrupted by storms or meteors, we are akin to clouds when travelling, so the feeling of being hit by something cannot be explained. I have asked since, but no messenger can relate.

When I arrived on earth, I found myself crumpled on the ground. I felt stiff, I couldn't get up.

By coincidence, or so I thought, it was the

homeless man that found me. The dying are never shocked to meet me, I think souls are ready whatever their age or circumstance, but the man was surprised to find me on the ground.

"Are you ok?" he asked.

I told him that I didn't know. I had never experienced anything like it. Was I sick? I don't think messengers can become sick. I must have been injured although I felt no pain.

The man helped me up and sat me on a bench.

The bench was strewn with his possessions, a blanket, a coat, a carrier bag with some bread and a small piece of cheese. There was also a crumpled photo of a child with his mother. Was that the man as a boy? I assumed he had been looking at the photo just before I arrived.

The man had seen me looking but offered no explanation.

"Can you drink?" the man asked.

I nodded as he offered me a flask. I don't know what I expected but it wasn't water. Still, it tasted wonderful. We can only eat and drink on earth, when we become whole for a short while, those opportunities are rare. I thanked him.

"If I had a home," he said "I would take you there, but I have not. You may sit here a while though, until you feel better"

I was desperate to ask how he'd ended up there, on that bench, but I sat in silence with the man with the kindest eyes as he shared his blanket and some of his bread with one of Death's messengers. What would the people think of the two of us? Should they be able to see me which, of course, they couldn't.

Four days and nights I had sat with the man. I felt weak, too weak to begin our journey, yet strangely glad to be there. Although the man hadn't shared any of his history with me, I did get the opportunity to watch how he lived, how he managed day to day.

The man was loved, not by family or friends, I never did get to the bottom of that, but by the local people. It seems that he had been there, living at that bench, for many years and people now considered him part of village life. Folks would stop to chat, and many would bring food and clothing to the man. In return he would do small jobs for them. One day I watched as he helped put up the stalls for the market and helped take them down later. The man would watch peoples' dogs for them as they shopped, carry heavy bags to peoples' cars, sweep shop fronts at closing time and clean windows. Even the children loved him despite his rather striking appearance.

I'd seen enough.

I decided that I would let him stay a while. I had convinced myself that his way of life would never impact too heavily on timelines as he was still a loner albeit a loved one.

"You can stay," I said in a grandiose tone that I regretted immediately. "I will return, of course, but I can grant you a warning. In return for your help these past few days I will send signs when your time is near."

Ten years passed but I would check up on him every now and then, just to keep an eye on timelines if I'm honest. Death was not impressed at my leaving him behind but, because of my impeccable work history and my assurances that all would be well, she had agreed to let it go if all other timelines remained intact. They had.

That said, I cannot tell you how relieved I was to receive word of his new death date.

"You told me that you would send signs!"

The man was cross. It was a surprise to see him so, I'd only ever seen his kindness.

"I did send signs," I explained "there was the near miss with that bus, the bout of flu that made you so poorly and the aches and pains signaling old age. I'm not sure how much clearer I could have made things"

The man's face was no longer kind. He said he

wasn't ready, that he'd never be ready.

"All this time I have been feeling guilty for what I did to you," said the man.

I was confused. What could he possibly do to me? I am Death's messenger, only she can do to me.

"I thought we had become friends, I thought you would leave me longer than these past ten years!"

I didn't know what to say so I just explained that I don't choose death dates, that is the work of the Calculators.

We stood in silence for a moment.

"I should have hit you again," the man said without remorse.

As I looked at him, angry and bitter, I realised that four days is not long enough to know a person. I had seen his kindness to others and assumed that his kindness to me was the same, but it was not, it was manipulation plain and simple.

I was a fool. I would not be a fool again.

That journey home was more than a little awkward.

Drink, Die, Live

By Nicola Warner

Drinking himself into a coma wasn't the best way to get a good night's sleep, but it was his favourite home remedy, one he had inherited from his mother. He would watch her when he was younger and often wonder why she would do it, why she would need to. Only now was he understood. Negativity has many forms, and it can overwhelm the strongest of minds. Once it struck the right nerve it would claw its way through burying itself deep.

Finding reasons to drink was a skill he had perfected. He drank like he was trying to drown tiny demons living within him, they goaded him, "come on, is that all you got? That's barely enough to paddle in!", the party wasn't over until the last demon had hit the floor cold. Even then in their drunken drowse they would still provoke the next shot.

He stayed in his bed, flat on his back, trying to slow the battering inside his chest with slow deep breaths. It was time he made a decision, it was either drink and die, or change and live. The advice the Doctor had offered swirled round dizzily in his head. He was slowly poisoning himself from the inside out. If he didn't stop now, it wouldn't matter who looked after Kara and the baby, he would just be a memory on a mantelpiece that they would refer to from time to time, "such a shame you never knew him," they will say as they rock the baby back and forth in front of his picture. Jed wouldn't give him a second thought; he would probably place the picture face down as he walked past. With him out of the picture Kara would be fair game, he could take her and the baby and be praised for stepping up when no one else would, "suppose I could haunt him, express my disapproval in the afterlife," he chuckled to himself.

Hello

by Nicola Warner

Hello? Can you hear me?

This line is so bad

It happened yesterday

I tried to call dad.

Hello? Can you hear me?

I'm here, can't you see?

I'm shouting so loud

But you can't hear my plea.

Hello? Can you hear me?

This line's getting worse

You're drifting away

I can't tell you, this hurts

Finally, I see you!

I made my way here

I just had to be with you,

I wanted you near.

Hello? Can you see me?

I'm standing right here!

I'm tugging your arm

I'm holding back tears

Hello? Are you there?

You've left me alone

I'm cold and I'm frightened

I just want to come home.

I saw you again

At the grave where you cry

You asked and you begged

For a reason why

I looked past your shoulder

And the name I read

Sent a chill down my spine

... It's me ... I'm ... dead?

Extracts

Monica

by Tricia Ramsay

It was a rainy day. Monica had just come in from playing basketball with a group of teenagers on their week's scheme. She knew the importance of physical exercise to help your mental mind-set. Not just from her own experience but also as a trained Youth Worker. She'd enjoyed the activity and after the first few days she felt she was seeing some 'cracks' in the hard armour of some of the kids. This wasn't just a job; this was her vocation and she never forgot she was lucky to be in this position.

She hadn't had the best upbringing and she could have, so easily, gone down the wrong route. Some would say, she did go down the wrong route. The fact she had been able to become a Youth Working despite her past, was an absolute fluke in itself. She had been through a lot. She could relate to the issues these kids were facing too.

She had always had a self-belief that she could turn a bad situation around into something good and worthwhile.

She walked back into her office and felt a cold shiver as she entered the room. Now she had stopped running around outside, her body temperature was dropping, enhanced by the dampness of her clothes and hair. She walked over towards her sports bag pulling out a towel to rub her hair dry. She quickly put the heater on in the office and then walked down to the toilets, to change into some dry clothes. As she returned, she put her wet damp clothes into a plastic bag, before putting it back into her sports bag and then put the kettle on. Which was sitting above her mini fridge, in the corner of the office.

Once she'd made herself a coffee, she sat back down into her office chair behind her desk and switched on her computer screen. She wanted to update her findings with each child before it was time to go home. As she was completing her reports, she saw an email coming through which wasn't work related. It was from Millie Campbell nee Davies. She was baffled for a few seconds and then realised there had been a Millie Davies from her school days. She was hesitant whether she should bother opening it. Looking back to the past, her school days hadn't been the best. She now knew she'd been groomed by a teacher, actually by more than one. That was a very dark time in her life and she'd been accused of being responsible for a female teacher's death. Back then, she was hurting so much, she was stoned most of the time, because it was easier than dealing with the reality of her shitty life. If someone told her, she was responsible for someone's death. She wouldn't have known whether she was or not, so accepted her fate.

The kids she worked with now, had harder things to deal with, with County Lines, street gangs, drugs, abuse, violence and stabbings. But she couldn't give up on them, not like society had done to her. That's what drove her to be the best Youth Worker in Ealing, she understood their pain and she was qualified and equipped to help lead them away from crime and show them, they deserved a better life. To help teach them, they deserved respect for themselves, the right way.

She took a sip of her coffee before opening up the email. She had been correct; it was someone from her school days. Inviting her to a school's reunion of '86. This could either be a good way to air out the cobwebs of the past, OR another excuse for people to point the finger and feel superior over her again. She'd learnt to never run away from problems and so with that vein in mind, she clicked on accept and it pinged back out to Millie.

She took another sip of her coffee. Thinking back to those days, Millie had been one of the nicer girls. Hopefully she was only going to invite the nice crowd instead of the ones who had pretended to be her friends, fake and manipulative, who took advantage of her. They had dropped Monica from a great height when she needed them most.

Monica took a deep breath, she wasn't that teenager anymore, she was a responsible adult who did good in society and who helped the youth of today, to prevent them becoming the youth she had been, back then.

New Beginnings

by Nicola Warner

A light tapping disturbed him mid-pour. He shot his eyes towards the annoyingly loud clock which hung off centre on the wall, "its bloody 9.45! Who the hell is that at this time of night? He huffed as if he was expecting someone to respond.

He unlocked the door and flung it open. His mother stood wearing a soft smile, "Can I come in?"

He nodded, and politely stepped aside.

"Sorry it's so late." She said as he closed the door after her. "I thought I should let you know that Kara went into labour, Jed's with her."

He rolled his eyes, "of course he is."

"They are waiting a little while before they head over to the hospital. I think you should be there too," she suggested as she studied his face.

"I really don't think that would be the best idea, would it mother? I'm the last person Kara wants to see right now."

"You're the father, you have as much right to be there than anyone."

"Do they know you're here telling me all this?" He questioned, raising his brow. He knew the answer as soon as she turned to him. She peered into his eyes, which made him shift and look away.

"What has happened has happened, we can't change the past." She told him, grabbing his face forcing him into an uncomfortable stare, "but we change set new paths for the future." She continued.

"I see therapy is agreeing with you mother." He laughed in a feeble attempt to change the subject.

"Cheeky sod." She laughed, slapping him playfully., "but seriously, I think it's time you all wipe the slate clean, especially with the baby."

He frowned at her, "I'm no good for that baby mum, they would be better off without me fucking up their life too."

"That baby needs you!" she assured him, "and I think you need that baby in your life a little more than you are letting on."

"I tried, Mum."

"I know." She reassured him, "let's put the kettle on, eh? We have a bit of time."

"Actually, I was in the middle of pouring myself a drink!" He laughed, but stopped at his mother's disapproving scowl, "... but I guess tea would be a more sensible option."

She returned a smile, "see, change is in you, it's a choice. You *will* get there."

"Thank you, Doctor." He smirked.

She rolled her eyes, "Oi, less cheek, more tea."

His mother's phone rang in her hand, he hadn't noticed she was holding it, she answered it in a hurry, "Hello? Jed? Is everything ok?" She paused, "Oh wow, ok. Moving quickly then, OK yes, I will meet you there. Bye love, bye!"

Her face beamed, she was very much looking forward to being a grandmother, a little squeal escaped her as she turned to Vince, "are you ready?"

Night of the game

by Paul Clark

The board was a large octagon. The four top guilds were at the stations of the wind. North, east, south and west. From each station a triangle stretched towards the centre of the board. The colours were bright. Yellow for the merchants, royal blue for the law, red for the butchers and green for the growers of crops.

As the teams started to come in the sound of boots on floorboards gradually resonated creating a boom which filled the main room and spread throughout the building, reaching all the corridors. The boom seemed to be calling to the townsfolk.

A parade lasted four hours with teams of men and women clad in their guild robes. All manner of carrying cases were brought in. Some were canvas but most were wooden and heavily stained but each had gold symbols painted on it.

Four armies had assembled. In this preparation time people were gathering in the balconies which reached to the ceiling. Everyone was quaffing from metallic vessels; a teal party atmosphere but the activities and actions which would follow will have potentially dangerous results.

As the clock struck its 12th chime the lamps around the room gradually lost their glow. Suddenly the playing board was brought to life. The sun had reached its zenith and over the years had been assured that the board was ready. The pieces of the glass mosaic had been turned during the previous six seasons.

Oooh filled the room. The three team members of each army were deep in discussion. Everyone was trying to whisper but the end result was a mass hissing: a mega nest of snakes.

They knew they had to find out how many more soldiers there were going to be and when they were due to arrive. Turk already had an idea of a welcome which they would not enjoy!

They needed to look at the plans on the parchment which the Reverend passed to his visitor.

They followed him and they noticed he was in deep discussion with one of his lieutenants.

"Follow my lead" Turk said , smiling. He beamed, eyes glinting with mischief.

The three of them walked towards the cloaked figure; they were deep in conversation. As they got level with him Turk shouted and cannoned into him hauling him to the floor. Berne and Jess rushed to help him. As Turk and Berne made a great show of removing non-existent specks of dust and checking for broken bones Jess , screened by the two big men, managed to look at the scroll and return it to its deep velvet lined pocket.

The "merchant " was clearly upset but he checked his pockets and realized that all was well and gave a deep bow before striding to the quay.

Back in the hall where they were safe from prying ears they realized they had a week to plan a most unwholesome welcome for a shipful of militia!

Turk already had a basic plan. They would use the sky carrier, a balloon filled with light air, to intercept the galleon. Confusion would be the key. Snakes and a few men would be perfect. Some of the bigger snakes could be trained in the time. His brow furrowed with the thought of snakes climbing down ropes from the sky carrier and nodded.

Time to start rolling these bullies back!

Santa Cecilia
Part i: The rain of blood
by Lewis Green

In the dungeons of La Guairá

David Casey awoke from fevered dreams to the sound of clanging iron. His mouth bitter from the blood still stuck to his teeth, the bridge of his nose bunged and pounding. The turnkey's baton rattled again against the rungs of his cell, causing his head to pitch and sway in nauseous momentum. Thinking his ordeal was finally over, he was now prodded this way and that as the shackles on his ankles dragged in the dust behind him. The ones on his wrists too tight, causing them to swell. He was led to a low doorway tiled above by blue and yellow mosaic. An oak door opened with a creak and he raised his hands to his eyes to shield them from the brightness of the room beyond.

"Siéntate señor Casey." Casey, still adjusting to the light peered through squinted eyes at the voice. "Siéntate," came the voice again, and a chair was pushed against his legs. He sat down stiffly and lowered his eyes to his lap, aware again of the sting from the wound above his nose. Casey regarded the man on the other side of the desk. His shirt sleeves were rolled up at the elbow and the man had a deep scar running from just below his left eye down to the line of his jaw.

"Midshipman Casey, if you don't mind," Casey cleared his throat and was surprised his voice came so clear.

At this the man laughed, "mutineers hold no title señor Casey, you know this."

"I am no mutineer."

"That remains to be seen."

"¿Dónde estamos?"

"Quite simply Midshipman Casey," the man smiled, "we are not far from where you landed. You will be here as our guest until we decide to hand you back to your *government*," the man took some time over this word, as if it pained him to speak it out loud, "until we get some satisfactory answers."

"*Answers*," Casey mused as if he had never heard the word before.

"And, if we don't get them from you, we expect to pick up Captain Pigot before long."

"Captain Pigot ... you really will need my help then."

"How so?"

"Captain Pigot won't be in any fit state to answer your questions."

"Dead?"

"Many times over."

The man smiled at this. Somewhere overhead cannon fire shook the foundations of the room in which they found themselves.

"Who killed him?"

"The crew."

"And how did it come to pass that you are still alive?"

Casey thought hard about this, "I was generally well respected amongst the crew ... they felt ... sympathy for me."

"And why should they show sympathy for you ... you were their ... how do you say ... *superior*?"

"Let's just say that Captain Pigot sometimes took his punishments too far."

"We had heard about Captain Pigot's methods," the man lit a cigarette, "how bad did it get?"

"See for yourself," Casey leaned forward in his chair to try to lift his shirt.

"Help him."

Two guards stepped forward to help him. As his shirt was lifted an imperceptible grimace passed his face.

The man inhaled through his teeth at the sight of Casey's back. "So you arranged for him to be killed, is that correct?"

"No ... I didn't have anything to do with it...I was tied up below-deck."

"What happened to the boatswain?"

"I don't know ... I can't remember."

"I don't believe you."

The man waved his hand in the air, "take him back to his cell." The man stubbed out his cigarette in a bowl on the desk in front of him, "... and send for the medic."

The medic, a man of around fifty, wearing a white cotton shirt yellowed at the collar and sleeves, stood outside the cell door and asked the turnkey to be let in. He rubbed a balm on the lacerations on Casey's back and applied fresh bandages to the wound, which were held in place with tape. He was then brought a clean shirt. The medic left the cell and whispered something into the ear of the man standing outside the cell door. Then the medic went away, leaving the man alone outside the cell.

"Think on what happened, Midshipman Casey ... I will still need satisfactory answers from you."

The man shut and locked the cell door and walked away along the corridor.

Casey now back in the cell he had left maybe an hour previously, before his interrogation, sat on the floor and rested his head between his knees. He had believed himself to be alone in the cell, but from the darkest corner came a cough. As his eyes adjusted to the light, Casey now saw a vague shape leaning against the wall.

"Excuse me sir, I fancied myself quite alone down here."

"Ha, do not apologise to me young man."

"What is your name sir?"

"My name is Franz ... and yours?"

"David...Casey."

"And you're a navy man."

"Yes, how did you know it?"

"What else would you be doing in this hellhole?"

"This is a relatively fair place in the world to my reckoning ... speaking of which, sir, where do you hail from? You are a German, am I correct?"

"You have a keen ear Mr Casey...I am from near Hamburg."

"How long have you been here?"

"What date is it?"

"September, twenty-eighth ... I think."

"The year ... what year is it? People in our situation should deal in years, not months or days."

"Seventeen ninety-seven"

"Then ..." the man mused, "I have been here for eight years."

"How have they been treating you?"

"About as well as could be expected ... the bastards at least had the decency to leave me with my pipe."

"Small mercies I suppose."

"Do you smoke?"

Casey nodded his consent and the old German passed over the pipe.

"Some good stuff there ... Turkish."

Casey took a drag from the pipe, coughed, and passed it back, "agreed, thank ye."

"What did you do to have been here for eight years?"

"Ha, let us not dwell on the past young man, let us think to the future."

"I'm not sure I can think too far into the future just yet."

"Maybe not, but I have a plan for *my* future."

"How so?"

The old man put his finger to his lips. At a nod of consent from his cellmate, the old man started to dig in the dirt beneath where he was sitting. After a while he held up a small knife, made dull with dirt.

"And what may I ask do you intend to do with that?"

"This, my young friend, is my key out of here."

"You'll ruin your chances of release."

"I'll never leave this place ... unless ... unless."

At the sound of footsteps in the corridor, the old German shuffled back into the darkness of the corner of the cell and soon after started to snore.

The night passed without incident and the old German stayed against the wall the better to conceal his makeshift hiding place.

Casey perceived it to be morning, not by the quality of light afforded the dungeons, but by the passing of hours. He heard a door open at the end of the corridor and the sound of footsteps. The footsteps came closer and stopped outside the cell door.

"Well, señor Casey, have you recovered your memory yet?"

"I'm getting there."

"Excelente, come with me."

The turnkey undid the shackles at Casey's ankles and helped him to stand. They walked along the corridor and entered the same office where Casey was questioned the day before.

"How are your wounds?"

"Better, thank you."

"Please sit down," the man waved his hand at the chair at the desk, "cigarette?"

"Por favor."

Casey looked around the room. His interviewer was the same man as before, and there were two men stood leaning against the wall smoking.

"There is one thing I do not understand señor Casey."

"Go on."

"Well, here is the thing ... your captain takes to punish you with the lash, a punishment not fit for a man of your status, and still ... and still you do not raise a finger against him," the man closed his palm in front of his own face, "or so you say."

"Because sir, I am ..." here Casey ran his tongue along his teeth, "I am ... English."

The man knowing not whether this was an insult or a statement of fact continued his line of questioning.

"Tell me then, what happened?"

"I will tell it to the best of my memory."

"Very well."

"It started about a week before the ... *incident*."

"*Mutiny* señor Casey, let us not pretend it was something that it was not."

"Well, Captain Pigot had noticed a loose reef knot on one of the sails that were the responsibility of the sailors that served under me. I took responsibility for this and Captain Pigot demanded that I get down on my knees and beg forgiveness ... which of course, I could not bring myself to do. So instead ... ," here a smile played across Casey's face, "so instead, he ordered me to be given twelve lashes. The men thought that my punishment was unfair ... *overzealous*."

"I tend to agree with them ... however ... this should not be enough to prompt *murder*."

"I believe their resentment had been brewing for some time. For a long time Captain Pigot had got into the habit of flogging the last sailor down from working on the top ropes."

"This I had heard from elsewhere."

"During a squall last month, three young sailors in a rush to not be the last man down, fell to their deaths onto the deck. Pigot had them thrown overboard. When the others complained, he had them flogged too."

"At which point did you know it was mutiny?"

"When I could smell the rum."

"You make fun señor Casey."

"I do not. Some of the crew had broken into the stores."

"Did you try to protect your captain?"

"I didn't get the chance ... I was pistol-whipped and had my hands tied behind my back and was thrown in the hold."

"Why didn't they kill you...like they killed the others?"

"I think I have already said that they had sympathy towards me."

"Ah, yes, now I remember," the man arched his eyebrows, "I wonder if you would grant them the same sympathy that they extended to you."

"Meaning?"

"Never mind, continue please."

"I'm not sure how much more I can be of assistance ... I was below-deck in the hold. I remember it had been raining and the rain came through the gaps in the planks. I heard the shouts, screams ... the sound of knives striking wood. Over and over again."

"What happened next?"

"I stood there in the hold waiting for them to come for me ... but they never did. I lifted my face to the ceiling of the hold ... I liked the feel of the rain on my face...oh god, I took it to be raining still ... but it was ... blood."

"What happened to the dead?"

"They were thrown overboard ... some of them still alive ... I ..."

"Bueno, señor Casey, there is no need to recount further ... we can guess the rest," the man lit another cigarette and passed it to Casey before lighting another one for himself, "the crew fearing that they would be captured, sailed here."

Casey nodded his head in assent.

"Alejandro, leave us for a moment ... head upstairs and fetch us some coffee."

Alejandro left the room and headed for a staircase at the end of the corridor.

"We have a job for you ... well not so much a job ... it is more like ... an opportunity for you to fulfil your *duty*."

"I'm listening."

"Quite simply señor Casey, I wish for you to track down the mutineers. After all you know all of them by sight."

"I do."

"If circumstance allows, you will capture them ... but if not ...," here the man looked through the window at the bay beyond, "well, then you will kill them."

Alejandro came back in with a tray of coffee cups and passed one to each of the men in the room, and lastly he took one for himself.

Casey sipped at his coffee deep in thought.

"Do I have a choice?"

"Why of course you have a choice señor Casey ... the choice is freedom, or ... well, to stay here in your cell."

Casey looked at the window.

"I'll do it."

"Excelente."

"I ask only one thing in return."

"Name it ... if it is in my power I will grant it."

"The old man in my cell. The German ... release him to me. He will serve nicely as my right-hand."

At this all of the men looked at each other and then burst out laughing.

"Señor Casey, you speak like a man imprisoned for fourteen years, not a mere four days."

"How so?"

"Surely you jest ..."

Casey's face betrayed no sign of a smile. The men around the room started laughing again.

"Señor Casey, there is no-one in your cell, only you."

"But ... I was speaking to him only yesterday."

"No you were not."

"I shared a pipe with him ..."

"You shared a pipe in your mind only."

Seeing the confusion on Casey's face, the man sat down next to him.

"There was once ... a man in your cell, a German yes, but no longer."

"Where is he?"

The man drew his finger from left to right across his throat, "he is in the graveyard of the sea."

"That is quite imposible."

"Impossible, no ... the old German tried to escape years ago ... how else do you think I got this pretty scar," the man traced a finger along the scar on his face, "Alejandro shot him in the head ... then we dropped him into the sea," here the man pointed through the window to a vague point on the horizon, "over there."

Casey looked through the open window to the ocean beyond.

"I'm not sure I understand."

"That much, señor Casey ... is obvious."

The man lit another cigarette. "We will permit you a small stipend to be used for food and board ... until your mission is *terminado*. Also, we give you the use of two pistols ... should they be needed," the man smiled, "Alejandro, bring Midshipman Casey his things."

"Well then. Where would you have me begin?"

To be continued...

Family

Dad Talk
by Paul Clark

I spoke to my father today
At the dawning of the day
A few worries on my mind
As I watched the weasels play

With feints and jumps
How's and bumps
A moving tapestry
Around the grassy clumps

I smiled and spoke about my aims
My books, work and games
He said not a word
On my time, many claims

Each point did I expand upon
Still he didn't comment on
The weasels had retired
Homeward to ramble on

My father is no longer with me
He is always by my side
He comes to me in my hour of need
To my own future I'll ride

Essential
by Tina Cooper

Things that are essential – A List Poem

<u>**Tina**</u>
Air
Water
A home
A job
Love
Notebooks
Bourneville
My kids
Pencils
Warmth
Clothes
Comfy shoes
A good hat
Outside
The sea
Ice cream
Chips
Jaffa cakes
Apple pies
Minced beef
Hills

<u>**Tina's Son**</u>
Choices
Happiness

<u>**Tina's Husband**</u>
Electricity

Fossil fuels
Food
Toilet paper
Travel
Jobs

Tina's Daughter
Friends
Xbox
Jurassic Park and dinosaur knowledge
TV
Family
Technology
Money
Laughter
Happiness
A funny brother

Jealous Father

by Nicola Warner

It was unfair. It was Cruel. And it wasn't right.

He knew he had done some shameful things in the past, but he was working hard to put those right. His relationship with his mother was strong, they had repaired so much of the damage he had caused, it was a relief to him that after everything, he still had her on side. She was so certain that he had it in him to turn his life around. He wanted that too. He wanted to make her proud. He wanted to make his daughter proud.

He was happy with the progress he was making, he made a silent promise to his daughter the night Kara went into labour that he wouldn't touch another drop of alcohol, and he had kept that promise so far, even though temptation called on a regular basis, he did his best to slide the bar over to ignore.

The relationship he had with his brother was still strained, he had to bite his tongue against the snide comments his brother directed at him every time he held his daughter. He knew he wanted a reaction out of him, that would give him the perfect excuse to kick him out and cut him off. He wasn't going to give him the satisfaction. He wasn't going to fuck this up too. He could take it on the chin, for now, after all Jed wasn't as innocent as he makes himself out to be. You would have thought he would have shown a little bit of gratitude for not telling Kara about the whiskey bottle incident. Whether he deserved it or not, he could cause his own trouble if he really wanted to. Maybe he should remind Jed of that.

He had to accept that his future with Kara was not going to be the fairy tale they had planned together, and he knew that the blame fell on him for that, he pushed her away when she needed him most. He was being punished in the most traumatic way imaginable, he didn't get to home with his daughter each night. Instead, his heart would break every other day saying his goodbyes as his own brother walked off with a smug smile, carrying his daughter in his arms. She would grow to share a bond with her uncle that she should have with her father. Jealousy burned inside him. He should get the same time to spend with her. It wasn't fair. Had he not suffered enough?

He had painfully adjusted to the reality of Kara and Jed's relationship; he would nearly go as far as to say he was happy for them both. As long as Kara was happy … But how happy would she be if she knew Jed more or less left him for dead that night? Or how skillfully quick he was with a whiskey bottle?

I think I've suffered enough, that's my daughter. He can't have her too.

Gothic

A Bedtime Story
by Lewis Green

Daddy, tell me a story…

I, Charles Perrault, am awakened from a colourful and distorted fug. A dream of my distant childhood. My pipe still clenched between my teeth has made an ache of my jaw. From where I sit, I can see the snow is still falling against the windowpane. At this rate we'll be snowed in by morning. My herbarium hangs from the rafter above my writing desk. Bushels of wolf's bane, belladonna, henbane; myriad potions to help me sleep. That lazy cur of a cat is asleep by the fire in a bundle of scarves as before. I check my ledger – what had I written before I fell asleep?

Homo homini lupus est.

Man is wolf to man. I am pleased I still remember my Latin – Jean-Baptiste taught me well. Did I have wine tonight? A red ring marks my garbled words…ah, how could I forget? – I broke a glass and pricked my finger. I must remember to sweep up the glass before my daughter wakes in the morning.

Daddy, come on, tell me a story – I can't sleep…

Her voice comes again, thin as a reed through the wall on which year after year, she marks her ever-increasing height with chalk. I wish I could stop her growing up, to keep her a child forever. I am glad she has woken me though. I was having a dream, a terrible dream. The same one I have had since I was as old as she is now. I, who am now in the winter of my thirty-third year. Every night I dream of the woodcutter.

Red stockings, full moon, red blood. When I was a child, I lived next door to a beautiful girl. The same age as my daughter will be soon. Every time I dream I re-live that night. Over and over and over again. I remember, like tonight, it was a full moon. She was led into the woods by the woodcutter that lived in our village – a giant of a man. I can imagine her fleet of foot, pale as snow beneath the moon's radiance. How the winter's chill must have puckered her white flesh. Her pale form stark against the dark earth. The shrill of the constable's whistle when they found her red stockings hanging from the tree. They never told us everything that happened in the woods, but whatever did happen ended with her head being lopped off with the axe. I remember scrunching my eyes against the terrible sight, but it was already too late. What haunted me the most was the pointlessness of it all, the pointlessness of everything. And the red stockings swaying in the breeze.

Whenever I wake from my terrible reveries, I feel the sting of tears and have to wipe my eyes before my daughter sees me and asks what is wrong. How could I possibly tell her of the horrors that await? If the wolf and the woodcutter are the same, where is she supposed to turn for help?

Daddy, please…

I can delay it no longer. When I get to her room she has the counterpane tucked up to her chin and she smiles at me. Eyes as green as apples, as innocent as a lamb.

I love you Daddy.
I love you too sweetheart.

Tell me a story to fall asleep to – a scary one, it's nearly Halloween.

Yes, my beauty. Try real-life for a horror story my love, I think to myself.

I take a breath and begin: *Once upon a time there was a little girl…*

She was asleep before I could finish the story. She slept, fitfully at first, but then settled down so still, so peacefully, in a way that I hoped would be everlasting.

The Church
by Nicola Warner

She had never considered herself to be religious, she wasn't
sure what she even believed in, she didn't know whether
her parents had even had her baptised, but she is always
drawn to this building. Every day, she would end up here,
it didn't matter which path she took, she would find herself
stood in front of the long, arched windows starring in awe,
while her dog impatiently whined by her side. She
supposed he didn't really care too much for stained glass
artwork, framed in the dark stone of the church. The
colours were vibrant, the detail was amazing, it was
flawless. She soon realised she had no idea what the
pictures represented, she just really appreciated it. It made
her think of the stained glass in *Beauty and the Beast*, that
could be where her fascination started. That's right, blame
Disney. Disney is the reason she is standing here in the
middle of a church yard, staring up at a window with a
frustrated dog tugging at his lead. Although the pictures
didn't feel as happy as they did with *Beauty and the Beast*,
they didn't scream a romantic happy ever after, but they
still drew her in.

A wave of sadness washed over her, sending
ripples down her back. She shuddered, well that felt a little
weird she thought to herself. She looked around, not a soul
in sight. It was silent, the wind whistled through trees and
fluttered the ends of her dog's long curly ears now sitting
with his snout in the air sniffing out the elements. She
suddenly became very aware that she was encircled by
gravestones. Anxiety cradled its arms tight around her
chest, she pushed back, come on, get a grip! You come here
every day; no zombies have come at you yet.

"Ok, Ok, you grump," she grunted at her dog who had just given her an 'I want to leave, like right now' bark, "we'll go now, ok?" she tickled the top of his head with the tips of her fingers, before glancing back at the window. "It is really pretty though, not your thing though, is it?" she said as her dog bounced excitedly at the movement of her feet, almost stumbling over his own busy paws. She giggled at him as they headed back down the road that led them here, no doubt they would both be led back in the same direction tomorrow.

Historical

A Student's Life 1966

by Martyn Kempson

Afternoon flicks in Camden Town

then up to the Heath for a little sit down.

Home to a tenement in Mansfield Road

Rooms crudely divided to increase the load

of students packed in at 3 quid a shot.

Registered landlord? Probably not!

Essays and study can dull the day

so out again so Jack can play

bar billiards and pints in an Archway pub

and all-night folk in a Greek Street club.

Regent's Park stroll and up to the zoo

Lots to see but nothing to do.

Typical student far too vocal

Not a tourist but not a local.

It's getting dark again and with legs like lead

all worn out so off to bed!

Good Times

by Bob Bootman

Telling kids about the 'old days'

Stuff that we all miss

Get bored as they don't understand

It's nice to reminisce

Top of the pops on telly

Starsky and Hutch's car

Checking out Charlie's Angels

Someone shot J.R.

Had to get up to switch the channel

Of which there were only three

No DVDs or streaming

Or overnight TV

Typewriters and trim phones

Pound notes and platform shoes

Supermarket green shield stamps

Richard Baker read the news

Pick 'n Mix at Woolies

Fruit Salads, Milky Bars

Curly Wurlies, Hubba Bubba

Marathons and Mars

Etch-a-Sketch and Spirograph

Were on your Christmas list

Clackers that might shatter

If not, they broke your wrist

Milkmen visited every house

Postmen delivered twice

The Corona guy gave you tuppence back

For empties, that was nice

Fluorescent Raleigh Choppers

Playgrounds on a tarmac base

Witches hat and roundabout

Rocking horse with scary face

We'd stay out all day playing

Might climb up on a tree

Use jumpers for our goalposts

Be home in time for tea

Good times and great memories

Wouldn't want it all revived

Just think that it was 'different' then

Not sure how we all survived?

Luton 1954

By Martyn Kempson

Terraced houses smoke stained black

coalman's bags of nutty slack.

Fifty children in our class

stick for the boy who's always last.

To cubs in a woollen balaclava

working mother, absent father.

Sisters sewing sailors' hats

making boaters from straw plaits

The Queen at Christmas visits the town

flags in the streets as the rain pelts down.

Worsted Shorts and a khaki shirt

chosen well to hide the dirt.

Saturday flicks at threepence a go

Batman and Hopalong make up the show

Ninepence for Woodbines smoked in the smog

then dizzily home to be sick as a dog.

Carnegie library, polish and books

a regime of silence and frosty looks.

Jelly for birthdays and carnation cream

bed by eight thirty and off to dream

of football, the match and Saturday's game

and visions of Wembley for the Hatters again.

Novel Approach

by Bob Bootman

I've written the first novel

The writing is quite strong

It's called 'The Tale of Genji'

About fifty chapters long

I am a female author

Murasaki Shikibu

I know what you are thinking

It's Murasaki who?

I'll be rich and I'll be famous

When you come and buy my book

I'll give up doing wifely things

Won't have to sew or cook

The only failing in my plan

Is one I must concede

It's the end of the tenth century

And no-one can fucking read....

Roman Rutland

By Paul Clark

The fields in Rutland hide a secret

Which has come to light

Showing a duel ancient

An heroic bitter fight

A mosaic uncovered

Telling the Mythical Tale

Achieves and Hector

The latter doth fail

A story started by Helen of Troy

Her face launched a thousand galleys

From a field in Rutland

Drama's returned to the Valleys!

The 'True' Story of Lego

by Bob Bootman

Lego was actually invented

Around 5000 years ago

The truth behind the Danish brand

Not many people know

Invented by a stone age Brit

To keep his children quiet

Following an inspired dream

In the middle of the night

He worked all through the morning

Drew his plans upon a slate

Little bricks to build a model

The concept bloody great

The Wiltshire folks not interested

His project off the rails

No locals here would back his plan

So he trundled off to Wales

He found a man near Newport

Who said he'd make the bricks

He left him with his drawing

And a model made of sticks

Thirty five years later

A loud knock upon his door

The bricks had been delivered

He was shocked at what he saw

A circle made of silcrete rock

But he'd got the scale wrong

Each brick was fucking massive

No surprise it took so long

The Stone age guy was fuming

And gave a bad review

He wanted all the stones removed

And all his cash back too

The Welsh man wasn't happy

Left the stones as his revenge

Refused to give a refund

And that's how we got Stonehenge

Then a Dane did visit Wiltshire

Around 1933

Made a Stonehenge model in plastic

That's how Lego came to be

Time of the month

by Tina Cooper

Some moons ago I took myself off to college to learn all about the Tudors and the Stuarts. I love me some history but I have the attention span of a toddler that has spotted an anything ever so was unsurprised to be awarded a U. This U did not mean Unbelievably Good. No. So disastrous was my exam that it went Ungraded.

The night before the exam we were given our expected grades, these were estimated upon the level of excellence in our work thus far, I was heading for a B+. Woo hoo.

I sometimes wonder if that was the lowest point in our tutor's life? Predicting a B+ only to discover that I was awarded a U. Was I his last ever student?

Not to worry, I hadn't gone to college to pass the exam, I was there only to talk about the Tudors because I was 24 and none of my friends were interested in Henry or any of his six wives. I'd had a ball but couldn't remember my own name once the Guard of the Exam had said "you may now begin."

Our tutor had, kindly, given us a small but perfectly formed heads up.

Should we get nervous we could head straight to question 50 which was always about witches. I was good with the witches, I'd got this.

I hadn't got anything.

There were three possible questions, two of which I knew like the tiny mole on the back of my leg and one that I did not. You 're probably ahead of me now and you'd be right, the exam paper wanted to know all the things I did not and none of the things I did.

Fast forward to results day and my mum heading off the postie to open the envelope addressed to me and, in the middle of the street, shouting "hoorah, my daughter got ungraded" then wandered into the house to pop my failure in pride of place on the mantelpiece.

Parents huh? They're proud if you do and just as proud if you don't.

My history course wasn't the waste of valuable drinking with my mates' time that my result would have you believe. No. Whilst there I discovered why women get such a bad rap.

Periods.

Ok, perhaps it's not as simple as that but still, we were once considered witches because we bleed for 7 days a month, every month, yet we refuse to die. Not only do we not die every month but some of us can go a little… erm…

a little bit… quirky at certain times of the month. Also, we women were considered to be less intelligent and as such more susceptible to sin. Girls just wanna have fun and all that.

In the good old days of yore, before science became the "in" thing, we humans did a whole lot of guessing.

We guessed that everything on our, then flat, planet was made up of four basic elements: earth, air, fire and water. Perhaps trees were 55% fire, 2% earth and 43% air but humans were 30% earth and 70% wind? I have no idea how it worked back then but I have found that, after watching Richard Hammond Builds a Planet, they weren't as far out as I first thought. That is for another day when I'm not so hot and sticky and can be bothered to have a Google but I remember many elements being involved. Personally I believe I am a mixture of gold, hot air and biscuits.

We also believed in spontaneous generation, that a life could grow from nonliving matter. For example; if you popped a sweaty shirt into a box of grain and left it for a few weeks it would turn into mice. (I watched a video somewhere) I daren't imagine where we believed babies came from. Oh, silly me, storks.

Before we understood we just made stuff up. Didn't understand a thing, no matter, it was probably magic or God or a little of both. Bad weather and ruined crops were the work of a disgruntled God. If you had a lazy eye or were unlucky in love then that was probably the work of the local witch. Should you be wealthy and handsome you'd probably done a favour for a fairy and so on.

Where was I? Oh yes, back to bleeding women.

I found the witch trials in Europe absolutely fascinating. Between 1560 and 1630 we really went for it and many witches, of all genders, shapes and sizes, were executed to stop them cursing your crops or your love life. These years were the busiest but witch trials had been plentiful before and continued to be popular for many years after.

We still have witch trials today only instead of the Malleus Maleficarum, the 15th century guide to spotting and executing witches, we have social media and internet trolls. Modern day witch hunts rarely end with an execution but many victims cannot show their faces in public again, get a job, nip to Starbucks or live happily ever after.

So, we women bleed a lot. In fact I was once told that I am a very good bleeder. I was in A&E at the time so I was rather chuffed as my nurse must have seen many bleeders in her time. I asked if there was a badge or something but alas I received nothing but a gentle rub of the knee. To be honest it was a lovely rub of the knee, it made me feel like a child again when she told me I was doing well. Would it be too much trouble for the nurses to keep a packet of stickers in their pockets?

Anyway...

What did women do with their blood? Historically I mean. We now have sanitary wear, towels and tampons, readily available and, in many places, free. Not in shops though, that would be bonkers.

I've had a little Google. What did we do before Google?

This is what I found from the Simple Health website, The History of Menstrual Hygiene. Dig in, it's more interesting than you think, honest.

3,000 B.C. - 5th century

Historians believe that Ancient Egyptians made tampons out of softened papyrus, while Hippocrates, Father of Medicine, wrote that Ancient Greek women used to make tampons by wrapping bits of wood with lint. Some women were also thought to use sea sponges as tampons (a practice still in use today!).

5th - 15th century

Women use rags as makeshift pads, leading to the term "on the rag" becoming slang for menstruation. During the medieval period there was a lot of religious shame surrounding menstruation. Blood is thought to contain the body's toxins and excesses, hence the use of bloodletting as a medical practice. Menstrual blood is considered dirty, and some even believe that drinking it will cause leprosy.

Another common belief? Burning a toad and wearing its ashes around your neck will ease cramps.

1822

The word "period" comes into use as a term for menstruation.

1850s

Women pin cotton and flannel into their bloomers when it's that time of the month. The sanitary apron is invented: a rubber apron with a strip that runs between the legs to prevent blood from getting on women's skirts and seats. They save furniture from stains, but they are smelly and uncomfortable. Menstrual belts—cloth belts onto which absorbent fabric can be pinned like a pad—came into use in the late 19th century, but aren't patented until 1922.

1896

The first commercially available pad hits the market: Lister's Towels. However, menstruation is still a huge taboo, so women don't want to be seen purchasing Lister's Towels, and the product ends up a failure.

1919

Pseudoscience on periods continues to get published. Professor B. Schick introduces the concept of "menotoxins", a name for the poison in women's menstrual flow that causes wine to spoil and flowers to wilt. Basically, men are still publishing Pliny's outdated ideas on real platforms in the medical community.

1920

French WWI nurses invented the modern pad when they use extra cellulose, a blend of acrylic cotton used for bandages, to soak up their menstrual blood. Kotex gets wind of the idea and develops a cellulose pad for commercial sale. Around the same time, Johnson & Johnson rebranded Lister's Towels as "Nupak", a name that won't betray their purpose with similarly elusive packaging. Pad sales finally take off (at least amongst wealthy white women who frequent department stores). Consumers take a box of pads and leave a nickel on the department store counter for total discretion.

1920s

Tampons are on the market, but they're applicator-free and quite leaky. Pads overtake tampon sales, boasting a "leak-free" solution.

1922

The menstrual belt is finally patented. Menstrual belts remain a popular method of menstruation management.

1930s

Leona Chalmers invents the menstrual cup: a rubber cup that stays in the vaginal canal and collects menstrual fluid. The first advertisements for the menstrual cup appear, but it's not a commercial success.

1931

A man named Earl Haas invents the modern tampon: cotton, applicator, and all. Haas gets the idea from a female friend who manages her period by plugging her vaginal canal with a sponge. The key invention for Haas is the applicator, which allows women to insert tampons without touching their vaginas or menstrual blood. As vaginas (particularly menstruating ones) still carry cultural and religious taboos, many women feel uncomfortable engaging with their private parts, so the applicator is a big deal. Kotex passes on the tampon because they don't think it will be a success. (Fun fact: a true ally to women, Earl Haas later invents the diaphragm, too.)

1933

Gertrude Tendrich buys Earl Haas's tampon patent and creates the company Tampax. Still, tampons are advertised to married women only, as people believe you can lose your virginity by using them.

1940s

O.b. Tampons are marketed as a smarter alternative to standard tampons with applicators. O.b. stands for "ohne binde" in German, which means "without napkins".

1969

Stayfree markets the first ever pad with an adhesive strip, putting an end to menstrual belts.

1975

Rely tampons hit the market. They're ultra absorbent, made of polyester and carboxymethyl cellulose. Unfortunately, these materials also breed bacteria more easily than cotton, and TSS awareness hits the mainstream. Rely tampons were recalled in 1980.

1981

Within the same month, two women are acquitted by British courts, one charged with murder and the other charged with intent to murder. The reason? PMS. (That's right, PMS remains a legal defense on par with insanity right up through the 1980s.)

1985

The word "period" is spoken out loud in a commercial for the first time ever by Courtney Cox, in an ad for Tampax.

2003

Lybrel, a continuous use birth control, is the first of its kind to receive FDA approval. Now women can skip their periods entirely, with federal approval!

2000's

Menstrual cups come back into fashion as an environmentally safe alternative to pads and tampons.

2013-2015

The trend towards more transparency and broader consumer awareness leaves an opportunity for direct-to-consumer companies like Cora, Lola and Sustain Natural to launch 100% organic cotton tampons (followed by other organic feminine care products). Women care about what they put in their bodies and are receptive to alternative options.

2016

Flex—a startup that sells new menstrual technology—introduces the menstrual disc. Menstrual discs differ from menstrual cups in size, shape, and fit in the body, but serve the same purpose. Flex raises over $1 million in funding within its first year. Feminine care and the public opinion towards menstruation has certainly come a long way, but there is still a long road ahead. Today, we optimistically watch as more and more individuals and organizations continue to push to dissolve the taboo in (hopefully) this lifetime—because women shouldn't have to wait another 5,000 years!

So there you have it. Thank heavens for copy and paste. I have taken away a few things from my in depth (no not really) research…

Firstly, wood with lint wrapped around it… ouch!

Secondly, sea sponges are still in use today… well I never… and I won't but still, that is a splendid idea. They are natural, they are absorbent and they are free. I assume they are free. Probably not now I think of it but they should be.

Thirdly, drinking menstrual blood will cause leprosy... who and why would anyone drink menstrual blood?

Fourthly, isn't the period fascinating? I think so. I think I would find them even more interesting if I wasn't 50 and still having them. Roll on the next weird stage of womanhood. Hoorah to all things menopause. Yay!*

*quietly sobs as she dips another biscuit in her tea

Inspirational

I asked Alexa for a song

by Tina Cooper

"Alexa, play me a song"

"Here is a station you might like, your soundtrack on Amazon"

For some reason Alexa chose Chic Le Freak. I have never asked Alexa for Chic Le Freak. I now sit here wondering why not?

I didn't have to sit and wonder for long. I had simply forgotten all about Le Freak, which is a shame because it is a fabulous wee tune. My friend Carole and I used to dance to this whilst singing into hair brushes, we were about eight I think. Oh to be eight, that would be lovely. Not forever, just a few days. I could climb trees without the funny looks from the boring grownups and watch Roobarb & Custard with a Chocolate Lovely. Thinking about it, I'll take a week in the 70s please.

I am struggling not to get up and boogie around the kitchen, the dog loves it when I have a boogie.

Sorry, predictive text, the dog gets worried and tries to stop me when I boogie but I cannot, nay, will not stop.

Oh, we're on to Jimi Hendrix now, Alexa knows me too well!

Jimi popped up in a documentary recently and I went a little Hendrix crazy. How the hell does a person forget about Jimi Hendrix?!

Can't sit still for this one, excuse me for a moment…

Oh, now we have Gone with The Wind Is My Love by Rita and the Tiaras.

What a tune! I love this song but wouldn't have a clue how to ask Alexa for it. Who are Rita and her Tiaras? I've never heard of them, till now and only then because I asked Alexa, the all knowing sage.

It appears that my soundtrack, courtesy of Alexa, consists of older tunes which begs the question, why?

No, she's lost me now, Love Her Madly by the Doors is dreadful. Sorry Jim.

"Alexa, play Sabotage by the Beastie Boys"

This is my favourite tune at the moment because it reminds me of the 2009 Star Trek film which then reminds me of my dad who would absolutely hate this song with every ounce of his being.

My dad, my son and I love Star Trek. The Husband and daughter are Star Wars fans so we no longer associate ourselves with those turncoats, we do not speak their names. Dad and I are and were fans of the original series and the shiny new films. I heard a rumour that there is to be a fourth film which is fabulous but makes me sad that Dad won't get to see it. Dad also missed out on Star Trek Discovery, he was quite poorly by then and didn't give a damn but I still think of him when I watch it.

My son, because he's 15, only likes the new films. I'm hoping he will continue the tradition and will come to the cinema with me when the next film arrives. It's that or I turn off the wifi.

I've wandered off, I'll ask Alexa for another song.

"Alexa, play me another song"

"You got it. Here's a playlist, 50 great Best of British"

Oh hell no! Heroes by David Bowie is not his best.

"Alexa, next song"

Go Your Own Way by Fleetwood Mac, I can work with that.

"You can go your own waaaaaaaayyyy"

Oooh, a little Amy Winehouse, nice!

Well, as much as I could happily sit here all day commenting on Alexa's choice in music like an out of touch X Factor judge, I must go. I'm off to the gym of all places. I am reliably informed by a PT friend that women of a certain age should strength train so thought I'd give it a go. It's horrible.

Please spare a moment to think of me at this difficult time.

I bid you a fond farewell as I leave you with the wise words of Captain James T Kirk of the USS Starship Enterprise.

"I hope your tribbles never trouble you"

Or something along those lines.

Looking for Interest in the Capital

by Martyn Kempson

Watch the lunchtime joggers

pounding the embankment

oblivious to the sun on the water,

domes, tourists, pigeons and beggars.

They preen with faintly superior air

eyes headlamp fixed, mouth open

cocooned by headphones.

they spring, sweat or gasp

as they seek to medal

somewhat in their imagination.

Nope
by Tina Cooper

I need to write
But I don't know what
An imagination
I have not got

An autobiography?
Then I needn't think too much
But I haven't done anything
Not yet, as such

Poetry then?
I wrote a corker called Foot
But that was a fluke
And I poem like I cook

What then?
It's just that I feel an urge
I might sit for a bit
Something might emerge

…

Nope

The Compleat Angler or

Hooked on a Writing Class

by Martyn Kempson

First ensure the swim is calm and weed free

taking care not to muddy the waters.

Prepare the lesson with literary ground bait.

Extracts of Maupassant, O Henry and Runyon

have proven effective in these waters.

Bait your barb with prospects of publication

and the worm of an idea and cast

gently into the bottomless talent pool

Watch intently for a ripple or splash of inspiration

in the chalk stream of consciousness.

At the right time strike

and reel the half-grown story

into the keep net where it can be admired,

deconstructed, and weighed in the balance

before being gently released to reach maturity.

Jobs

Duxford's Secrets

by Bob Bootman

Matthew's pace increased as he crossed the floor of the aircraft maintenance area. The smell of grease took him back to his school metalwork class.

He hated metalwork. Hated the whining of the lathes, the sticky Swarfega sliding through his fingers, tiny shards of steel splintering his skin, but, most of all, he hated Mr McDonald.

What a Bastard.

To get your attention, all the other teachers would throw chalk or board rubbers at you. Mr McDonald would throw Allen keys, screwdrivers, small hammers and you knew that you'd got a swipe on the arse from the aptly named "Bastard File".

He was a sadistic fucker and Matthew was shit scared of him.

Hurrying to escape the memory, he could feel his heart beat faster and beads of sweat forming on his forehead as he raced to get out, before a Scottish voice would boom his name and a small metal object came flying past his ear.

He finally reached the entrance of the Airspace Hangar and drew breath as he recovered from his mini panic attack.

He surveyed the fleet of retired aircraft surrounding him.

The Vulcan Bomber with its humungous triangular wings, a Harrier Jump Jet, seemingly halfway through a vertical take-off and a sleek, grey RAF Tornado.

All classic aircraft in their own right, but then, across the room, his eyes fell upon the most beautiful Aeroplane ever built. His teenage crush.

Concorde.

Matthew loved that plane and it wasn't Concorde's fault someone left a piece of metal on a Paris runway.

If it wasn't for that it would still be flying now.

He was so proud of the fact that Uncle Ron, an Engineering Draughtsman, helped to design Concorde and when Matthew saw all the drawings, he wanted to become a Draughtsman as well.

As he grew older though, he realised Uncle Ron was the most boring man in the world. Someone who could make a five-minute monologue last an hour. He would tell you his exact route he'd taken to drive to you and then the reasons why he didn't take the other routes. If he had a social media profile now, he would list his favourite pastime as the slow, but steady, growth of grass. It was only when he died that Auntie Barbara found an old briefcase hidden in a wardrobe, and discovered that throughout his married life, he had worked for the Intelligence Services.

He probably wasn't boring at all. That was just a ruse. He was leading a parallel life. All those "business meetings" he had to attend in New York and Bahrain, when he used to tell Matthew how he would travel on Concorde, flying at supersonic speeds, drinking champagne and having Fillet Steak dinners. They weren't business meetings. He was going to steal secrets or kill a spy!

Uncle Ron was the reason he was at Duxford.

In his will he'd left an envelope addressed to Matthew. In it was a piece of paper which just said

'If you want to drink Dom Perignon Champagne and eat Fillet Steak for the rest of your life look under the A12'

The rest of Matthew's family had speculated what it meant, and wondered if there was a massive bag of cash hidden under the road that runs from the Blackwell Tunnel, all the way up to Ipswich.

But Matthew knew exactly what it meant, and now he was standing at the bottom of the steps of Concorde and his heart was just about to go Supersonic.

All he had to do was discover what was hidden under seat number A12.

His legs grew heavier as he climbed the metal steps, relieved that no- one else was around, although not surprised, as it was late Tuesday afternoon, just before closing.

He glanced around the Hangar to confirm he was alone before he made his discovery.

Uncle Ron would have wanted him to make the revelation alone.

Entering the aircraft, he looked to the left, through to the cockpit, shocked at the wall of archaic dials and switches, the pilots would have expertly navigated on each flight.

No wonder they needed a degree.

Nowadays, Matthew felt it was likely your pilot

would be more qualified in virtual reality gaming than in aeronautical engineering. It seems the computer flies the plane more often than the pilot.

He turned and faced the cabin.

It seemed a lot smaller and more cramped than he remembered. At six foot three, he had to stoop slightly as he made his way through to his destination, maybe his destiny?

Subconsciously counting out loud, he reached row 12. Seat A12 was by the porthole window to his right. He checked again that he was alone and settled into the plush, leather upholstered seat. It sighed as air expelled from it. He imagined his uncle doing the same, maybe a few months before he died, maybe a few years?

He hoped Uncle Ron would be proud that he 'cracked the code' and was about to perform the 'pick up' Matthew took a couple of deep breaths to calm himself, his heart was still racing, as he thought, "this is it". He leaned forward and reached underneath the seat, his hand sweeping around the floor. The cold steel brackets of the frame was all his searching fingers could find, then his palm brushed over a sharp protrusion and punctured his skin.

"Shit, shit, shit" he winced, as blood started to ooze from the wound.

He pulled out a couple of tissues and compressed them against his palm to stem the flow. Then clenched his fist tight and tried to ignore the minor inconvenience, as he had more important things on his mind.

He flicked his phone torch on and got on all fours to continue the search.

He scanned under A12. Nothing. There was nothing under B12, nothing in front, nothing behind. Had he got it wrong?

Had he misinterpreted the message?

Matthew was so engrossed with his search, he hadn't noticed the figure standing in the aisle adjacent.

"Looking for something?" the old gravelly voice questioned. Matthew was startled. He banged his head on the underside of the seat as he struggled to rise up and face the old, smartly dressed gentleman. His eyes re-adjusted, focusing on the man. He stared, open mouthed, ashen, as though he'd seen a ghost. He thought he had.

"What the fu...you died, you're dead, I went to your funeral" he gasped. His uncle stared back at him, eyes glazed.

"I'm sorry Matthew, I very nearly died, I was poisoned. We had to make it look like I died, so we can go after the people that did it. They don't know I survived.

That's why I brought you here. I need your help to catch them."

To be continued….

The Builders are Back

by Bob Bootman

First thing in the morning

A new day is dawning

Half of them yawning

The builders are back

"Give us the key

We'll be done by three

How about some tea?"

The builders are back

Banging and crashing

Booming and bashing

Pounding and smashing

The builders are back

Digging and drilling

Cementing and filling

Sawing and milling

The builders are back

Lining and skimming

IPhones are ringing

Swearing and singing

The builders are back

Engines are roaring

Gas pedals flooring

Calm is restoring

The builders have gone

And breathe......

The Lament of the Allotmenteer

by Martyn Kempson

So much for the allure of grow your own

My patch is like a warzone

My tomatoes blacken overnight

From wind Bourn tomato blight

Pests attack my brassicas

Like Texas Chainsaw Massacre's.

I dig and hoe and weed til Dawn

But still my sweetcorn is stillborn.

My spuds are dud, my leeks are weak

Eaten by mice or pigeon's beak

I've given up, me efforts token

Blistered hands and spirit broken.

My fruit are wrinkled, they look like mingers

I just don't have ten green fingers.

The Launch Party

by Tricia Ramsay

This week had flown by so quickly, Tilly had moved out of her flat on Wednesday and Simon moved in on Thursday. I'd helped him finish getting settled in once I was back from work. He'd cooked a meal for us as a thank you. He seemed quite settled and luckily his neighbour, Mrs Baker, had agreed to pop into his house and feed the cat once a day. We found out that Sydney was a frequent visitor to Mrs Baker during the day anyway, so if he missed human company, he could always pop back to hers.

Whilst I was glancing around his temporary rented apartment, I noticed he had a laptop on his sideboard. If he was working from home, I'd be able to access some of the information from it later. Simon came out with two plates of lasagne and a salad. We sat down at his dining table and tucked in.

"Have you had any more thoughts on what was really going on with your mugging, phone tapping and the house break-in?" I asked, as I was picking up my glass of water.

"Not exactly. Individually they could be 'a bit of bad luck'. The phone tapping, I don't have 100% proof on, but I had a gut feeling something was wrong. Or it could be a bit of paranoia creeping in," he confessed, before taking another mouthful of food.

"I believe in trusting my gut feelings, what's yours telling you?" He sipped his water before replying. "My gut is telling me it could all be a coincidence apart from the fact that the words spoken by the mugger were the same words written on the note left at my house. There's got to be a connection," he said, shaking his head and looking thoughtful. " For the time being, all my other files I'm working on, I'm doing in the office. But on this big contract, I've got into the habit of using my mobile to make calls and doing the work on the laptop" he said.

"That sounds like a good plan of action," I said, and he smiled in appreciation as we continued to eat. I've actually called the "owner" to arrange a meeting to discuss a few points" he said, and I stopped chewing and looked over to him "we're meeting up tomorrow" he announced. I raised my eyebrows in acknowledgement.

Friday had started out well. I had booked half a day from work, as I was going to meet up with Amber for lunch. We would pick her luggage up from the locker at the train station and continue heading back to my home.

As always, she looked immaculate; she was groomed, to an inch of her life. God forbid she'd have a hair out of place. She thrived on looking perfect. To be honest, it was far too much effort, for my liking. I really couldn't be bothered about what people thought of my appearance. I let my work speak for me. But in her line of business, self-image was everything, and she'd used it to help her make a lucrative business for herself. This latest contact was only going to help her move up the social media ladder even further.

I admit, it was good to see her, we'd not seen each other for well over a year. Throughout lunch, she was explaining how her meeting had gone. Half of it went over my head, but I knew she'd sealed the deal and was really excited about the future. At the launch party tonight, the owner of the Company was also going to be there, and she wanted to leave a lasting impression on him. Ruthless in her pursuits, she'd 'get her man'.

I'd forgotten how successful and influential she'd become. But it was brought to the forefront when we were interrupted at our lunch by a "Fan" who recognised her from YouTube and Instagram and asked for a selfie. I offered to take the photo for them. Partly I was being supportive of my sister's fame, partly I was being kind, but also, I wanted to make sure I wasn't accidentally in the photo.

When we got back to mine, Amber did her "Amber inspection" of my new home, before she went into the spare room and unpacked her luggage. I swear, if you'd seen the size of the case, you'd think she was staying for a month, not one night. I made us a light dinner around six o'clock and by eight-thirty, we'd washed, de-haired and dressed for the launch party. We'd booked the cab for eight-forty-five.

I tried my best to get away with as much as I could to feel normal, but Amber had insisted I allow her to do my hair and make-up. Then she saw what I was going to wear and said, "Hell no!" and put me into one of her outfits. The thing you need to realise is that she is very tall, and her legs go "all the way up" to her armpits whereas mine aren't and don't.

So, my only Godsend was the mini dress she gave me, was a lot lower on me instead of it being at the upper thigh level. The rest of it worked and looked good. I quite liked the one strap dress, it had a big circle section missing from the side and around the back. It was a metallic purple; it suited my colouring.

As we got out of the cab, we walked straight past the rest of the "wannabe" crowd who were lining up in front of a couple of bouncers. I heard some of them call out Amber's name in recognition. Amber being Amber turned around and waved at them, then continued to walk over to a member of staff at the front desk, handing over our invites. The woman looked at it and checked it against a list on her screen. Then looked back at us and smiled. "If you wouldn't mind waiting a second, I'll get staff to escort you to the VIP area," she said. How the other half live, I thought.

A well-dressed staff member came over and walked us to one of the three lifts. He used his key card to access the top floor on the lift panel, and we went up. As we approached the top floor, I could hear the music. As the doors opened, it bombarded my senses with loud music, laughter, and fake smoke, which was dry ice.

The base of the music was pounding in my chest, overtaking my heartbeat. My natural thought was I had no place being here. I felt out of control, and I could feel my anxiety building up. I took a deep breath and followed Amber, walking over to the bar.

We got a glass of champagne and as we turned round Amber met someone who'd been in her business meeting earlier on in the day. His name was Spencer "something" and he escorted us over to a very oversized seating area and there, sat down with women all trying to catch his attention, was someone very important to Amber. But someone who I'd vowed I never EVER wanted to lay my eyes on again, Stephen Kingsley.

He looked up as Spencer introduced Amber to him and he smiled "so this is my new protégé. I've heard good things about you Amber". He stood up in his expensive suite and took her hand and kissed it, then took a side glance at me. "Stephen, I'd like to introduce you to my sister Larna," she said with a big smile on her face.

He put his hand out to take mine, but I declined the offer "So Larna, are you involved with social media too?" he asked "No!" was my reply. I wanted to get away. I leaned in and spoke into Amber's ear "sorry I just need to pop to the loo" and before I went "have I met you before?" Stephen asked with a frown on his face. I forced myself to smile "I don't think so, maybe I just have one of those faces" before pulling a funny face "I'm sure I would have recognised you, if we had" massaging his ego. "Please excuse me for a moment," I said and then dashed off to find the ladies' toilets. I could hear Amber apologising for me, as I left and then getting into her sales pitch of sucking up to the man. I took one quick look back to see she'd moved closer to him. They sat down together, ignoring every other person in the area.

As I walked away, I could feel my heart racing, and I needed a moment to calm down and think things through logically. I thought after a year my feelings of dread and fear would have disappeared, but no. I walked into the toilets and sat in a locked cubicle, focusing on my breathing and then opened my clutch bag and took out a tablet. These were prescribed meds for my anxiety, which I hadn't needed to use in ages. Luckily for me, I'd had the foresight to know a busy party with people I didn't know could set me off and I had brought some tablets with me.

I took the tablet with the help of the Champaign I still had in my hand and then closed my eyes." How am I going to get out of this" I kept saying to myself, when what I was actually saying was "fuck, fuck, fuck" I hadn't realised I'd been saying it out loud until I heard a knock on my locked toilet door "hello, are you ok in there?" it startled me, as I didn't recognise the voice "yeah I'll be out in a minute" I answered. I looked at the glass in my hand and downed the rest of its contents before pretending to flush the toilet and open the door.

I walked over to the sink and put my clutch bag down, then looked at myself in the mirror. I almost didn't recognise myself. Amber was good with makeup. It was me, but not me. I had to hold on to the fact that if I wasn't sure; it was me, that's why he hadn't been sure either. I couldn't allow my sister to be alone with that man, but if they stayed in the crowd, I'd be able to keep her safe.

The Stephen Kingsley I knew always has a bodyguard close by and I knew if I could trick Stephen into thinking he'd been mistaken about knowing me, I wouldn't be as lucky with his bodyguard.....Frank Mancini.

As I was waiting for my meds to kick in, I thought it safer to stay in the ladies, so I took out my lipstick from my bag and reapplied. As I did so, I was still staring at myself in the mirror, and I had a flashback to what had happened a year ago.

It was uncomfortable going back to what had happened, this wasn't the time to freeze in fear. I had come a long way since then, with my recovery, and I needed to have my wits about me. As I came out of my daze, I could see the ladies' toilets were getting busier. I stepped away from the sink and filtered through the line and back out into the party room.

As I came out of the ladies, a big built guy walked past all suited and booted. As I watched him from behind. I picked up the scent of his aftershave, which was lingering. Why did I recognise that scent? As I looked closer at his walk and stance, I realised he was someone from the past too and I felt my stomach do a flip. It was Frank Mancini.

Scratchings from a Writing Class

by Martyn Kempson

We are free range and freelance.

High tailed and long combed hens

Silver, grey and gold in abundance.

and three cocky roosters all flash and sound.

We fly to our perches

settle in pecking order

greasing our feathers against

the wet of critical opinion.

Heads down for a grain of inspiration

we come running for a treat

from the teacher's hand.

Kids

Vince and the Baby

by Nicola Warner

"You have got to be kidding me, Kara!" Jed groaned, "Was it not bad enough that he was at the hospital uninvited … are you ok with this? My mother didn't really give you a choice, just showing up with him like that," he paced round the kitchen, stopping abruptly at the kettle, he tapped it to life, and took two cups from the cupboard above, he assumed Kara would want one if he was making it.

Kara smirked at the sight of him by the kettle, him making tea was a rarity, "Finally, you're picking up on my telepathic waves!" she laughed, "I knew we'd get there!"

Jed shot her his unamused eyes and darted tea bags into the cups.

Kara sighed, "look your mum is right, if she can forgive and forget, the least we can do is try. We're not innocent in this either. I know you don't like hearing it, but he is her father, she deserves to know who he is."

Jed didn't answer, he was concentrating on mixing the concoction of tea and milk, spilling it over the sides.

"Jed, you're making a mess! Is there anything left in those cups? Don't you dare hand me half a brew!"

"Oh, sorry," he stopped and handed a cup to Kara.

They both shot their eyes towards the door as soon

as they heard the dainty tap if his mother's hand on the glass panel. Jed sighed.

"I'll let them in." Kara offered.

"Oh Kara, I was beginning to wonder if you had heard me, I didn't want to wake baby."

Kara smiled and stepped aside.

"Hi … these are for you." An awkward Vince handed Kara a colourful bouquet.

"Oh," she blushed, "thank you, Vince."

They made their way towards the kitchen, Jed had disappeared leaving his cup lonely on the countertop, "she must be awake," Kara smiled, "I'll go check." She placed the flowers in the sink and disappeared upstairs.

"Are you ok?" his mother whispered.

Vince nodded.

"Flowers were a lovely idea, well done."

They could hear Jed and Kara's muffled words, with a final hushing from Kara as they entered the kitchen. Jed had his arms folded and had the look of a toddler that had just been told he couldn't have any chocolate cake until he finishes his dinner.

"Look who's awake!" Kara beamed, "say, hi everybody!" she said in an almost muted high-pitched tone.

"Would you like to hold her? You didn't get to at the hospital."

Jed gave an uneasy stare as Kara placed the baby gently in Vince's ready arms.

"Watch her head."

Vince stiffened instantly, not wanting to do anything wrong, "I got her."

"Vince, maybe you should sit down with her." Jed's voice bellowed in the silence.

"Jed!"

"What? It was just a suggestion!" He smirked, "didn't mean anything by it."

"I'm sor-"

"You know, I think I would feel better if I sat down with her."

"Ok, let's go into the living room."

Jed watched closely as Vince followed Kara and their mother, not keeping his eyes off Vince and the baby. Vince took the seat he came to first, with Jed not far behind holding out his arms at Vince's unexpected manoeuvre.

"Tea anyone?" Kara asked cheerfully, and pulled at Jed's arm as she walked back towards the kitchen. "Jed!" Kara retraced her steps to usher him away, "give him a break, let him have some time with her."

"I'll go see if they need help," His mother winked.

Vince stared down at the silent bundle who looked back at him with deep eyes and a permanent frown. "Uncle Jed doesn't like me very much," he shuffled around the armchair, "should we try that rocking chair in the corner?" He carefully stood, not taking his eyes off her, and made his way over to the chair in the corner. He settled down, still watching, and began to gently rock them both, "ah that's better isn't it."

He watched as she started to fuss, his heart almost racing, he shushed her softly, her eyes drifted. She was sleeping soundly in his arms, he couldn't help but smile, not only with relief, but he couldn't believe how lucky he was in that moment.

Jed made his way into the room shaking a bottle, "I'll take her now, she's due a feed."

"But... she's ...erm... sleeping?" crap. Maybe I should have stayed in that uncomfortable tub chair. He watched as Jed screwed up his face, ready to explode at him.

"Jed didn't I say to give it a moment!" Kara huffed as she stormed into the room.

"yea, but .."

"Leave them!" she scowled as she dragged him

back into the kitchen, "I'm sure she will let us know when she is ready for a feed, and I think it would be nice for Vince to feed her."

Vince looked back down at the cosy bundle, "would you believe me if I told you that me and your uncle were close once? Thick as thieves, your nanny would say we made a good team. Sure we had our moments, we fought, we're brothers, but we were always there for each other when it mattered. Or when it mattered for me I guess. Your daddy can be a little selfish, but at least I'm pretty," he chuckled to himself, "your uncle got the brains, that's how he got your mummy. He tricked her with his deceitful tactics!" he fashioned a low evil laugh, "don't tell him I said that will you?" he whispered.

He sat quietly with her, rocking slowly, taking in everything – her smell – her button nose –the shape of her face – the little fuzz on the top of her head, "not very sociable are you?" he smiled, "you know, if daddy hadn't been such a numpty, things could have been different."

Tubthumping

By Bob Bootman

Our daughter was born at home, on our living room floor, at 1am on 2nd May 1999.

It was a planned home-birth, in the presence of our two midwives, Julie and Julia.

All had gone swimmingly, and, after a good few hours intense labour, our little bundle of wrinkled flesh popped into this world......grey and totally lifeless.

Our midwives worked swiftly. One trying to revive her, searching for a heartbeat, while the other on the phone calling an ambulance.

I knew it must be bad and just stood there, feeling helpless, while my wife, Gael, was lying on the floor, confused as to what was happening around her.

After working through previously practiced procedures, a faint heartbeat was detected.

They fought to keep our baby alive, helping with her breathing.

Our five-year-old son, George, was upstairs and our neighbour, Liz, was summoned to look after him, as we were rushed to hospital.

I say we, but when the ambulance arrived, I was bundled into the back of it, with our daughter, whilst Gael, being a second 'patient' had to wait for another vehicle.

I thought I was taking my daughter to die, without my wife, who was distraught and in a total state of shock.

I sat in the back of the ambulance numb and staring, while the paramedics connected cables and sensors to our fragile bundle.

Halfway to the QE2 hospital, the paramedic advised me that heartbeat had shot up to 140, which was a good sign and she was putting up a fight.

I phoned Gael to update her and give hope our baby will be okay and I'll see her at the hospital soon.

She just sobbed.

The ambulance arrived at the A&E doors and we were ushered into the emergency room to, what seemed like, a dozen Doctors, Nurses and medical staff, who sprang into action, hooking our baby up to various machines, as I stood by, keeping out of the way.

I noticed a young nurse giving me a concerned, pitying look from the other side of the room, as if to say "Poor bloke, wonder what is going through his head?...."

After a while, Gael was wheeled in, looking extremely forlorn and we watched for a while, not really knowing what was going on.

We were taken to a room, which had a bed for Gael, while they continued their assessment.

A Doctor visited and assured us that our 'little fighter' was still fighting and they were doing all they could to keep her going.

They believed our baby had her umbilical cord around her neck during the birth, thus restricting blood flow to the brain. The blood sample taken was quite toxic, confirming the lack of oxygen and we were advised to prepare for the fact that, if she did survive, it was highly likely she would have suffered some form of brain damage.

It was touch and go for the next couple of days and we even had her christened, Eleanor Julie (just in case she didn't pull through). When the Vicar touched her forehead with the 'holy water' her body convulsed, which was a bit spooky.

I wasn't allowed to stay overnight at the hospital with Gael, so would drive to and fro to the hospital several times a day, whilst trying to make everyday life as normal as possible for George at home.

Each time I turned on the car radio, the tune "tubthumping" by Chumbawumba seemed to be on and I'd singalong to keep my spirits up.

Taking George to school was weird, as I knew other parents would have been aware of our situation. I felt like eyes were upon us, but no-one approached me, preferring the English tradition of avoidance, rather than broaching the subject and offering support.

A couple of days later, Eleanor was off the ventilator, getting stronger and improving by the hour. Gael even started breast feeding. Something she steadfastly refused to do for our son!!

At six days old and after several tests, including an MRI brain scan, Eleanor was given the 'all-clear' to go home.

Nothing ever seemed to come of the predicted brain damage and her ten 'A' (and two "A' *) grade GSCE's are testament to that.

She is now at Manchester University, studying 'Humanitarian aid and Disaster Management', as well as learning Arabic on the side.

'Tubthumping' is our anthem and every time it plays, we jump around and singalong.

It reminds me of my trips to and from the hospital and, however bad things seem, there is always hope.

"I get knocked down, but I get up again, you are never going to keep me down"

We feel very lucky that she pulled through….

Ps Here is the poem I wrote for Ellie's 21st Birthday in 2020

Ellie 21

'Twas early morn', when you were born,
In Nineteen Ninety Nine
You came out grey, on the second of May
And extremely far from fine

But you battled hard, right through each yard,
Every ounce of strength you'd give,
The curve reached its peak, by the end of the week
And you won your fight to live

You grew up strong, and it wasn't long,
Before George became your bitch,
He did all you said, or else he'd be dead
And dumped right into a ditch

To us you were mean, when you were a teen,
We could never do anything right,
But then came a change, we thought it was strange,
When you watched TV that night

That Love Island appeal, it made you feel,
That you wanted to help the needy,
You turned on the bankers and big fat cat wankers,
Who were guilty of being too greedy

So you lived in a chalet, on the coast in Calais,
Helping guys who were living in tents,
Through the wind and rain, you kept going again,

And all at your own expense

And soon we will see, you with a degree,
In Humanitarian aid,
And we'll be so proud and shout very loud,
That our daughter is making the grade

But don't forget to have fun, coz you're twenty one,
And life is for living for sure,
Enjoy your time on this earth, for all that it's worth
And live it a little bit more

xxx

Love

For Bobby's Plant ... some love ...?

by Bob Bootman

That plant is looking very sick
It's leaves are turning brown
If it was a dog and I was a vet
I'd have to put it down

by Paul Clark

Oh for a drop of water
That Ficus would stir
Into leaf and life
How people err

So a drop not a dram
Would bring life again
Light up the room
And give oxygen!

by Tina Cooper

Is it really for the bin?
To the bin should it go
When all the wee thing needs
Is a little water to help it grow

Those who stayed

by Lewis Green

Now if you listen closely

when the door is held ajar,

you will hear the tap-tapping

of the umbrellas as they meet

the window.

The condensation forms drops,

leaves tracks down the glass

marking the passing of time

my love.

As does the yellowing of the

postcard kept in my shirt

pocket over my heart

my love.

Cherbourg is grey today, clouds

roll in and I watch the plash

and patter of rain, same as the day

your train rolled away.

Valentine's Day

by Martyn Kempson

We seek comfort in remembrance

moulded to fit our present needs.

The perfect day, the endless summer

pulls at strands of memory

stretched, ghosting as the filigree

of a spider's web, perfect yet fragile

and broken with a twitch of the synapse.

Magical Realism

Emerald Stone

by Tricia Ramsay

There has always been an element of mystery to Greyson's House, which was built on a vast Scottish estate back in 1820 by Reginald Greyson for his young and beautiful wife Isabella, who was Eastern European. Unfortunately, they were never blessed with children and Greyson had become disillusioned in life. After a cascade of bad business choices, he fell into despair and desperation, turning to drink and gambling. During these dark times, he fathered a child out of wedlock with a young maid working for them and Isabella had, had a hand in removing the girl and chose to bring up the baby as her own. The child was a girl and Isabella named her Sylvana and started teaching her, her old family ways from her mother land.

Isabella brought over a governess from Moldavia to educate Sylvana to a high standard, but also in the ways of witchcraft. Isabella slowly but methodically coerced the girl to despise her father and eventually he became more and more unstable. Some said he'd gone mad and disappeared. Isabella said he'd gone travelling to find himself and to recapture his business successes. But after a bitterly cold winter, several months later, one of the grounds men found his dead and decomposed body hanging from one of the trees in the vast forest on the estate.

Isabella had quickly decided she needed to find a way to bring some income. So, she turned the house into a boarding school for girls in 1829.

As an adult, Sylvana became a teacher herself and taught young girls a standard of Education, etiquette and Witchcraft.

***

Penny Quigley was the Head Teacher of this very prestigious boarding school, in the outer regions of Scotland. It was well respected, almost legendary, as a finishing school for the daughters of Nobility and aristocrats. It was gothic in design as it had been built in 1820. Of course, in these modern times, there were more celebrities' children creeping through the doors. If they could pay the school fees, so be it. However, the school had learnt many years ago to be more selective with who would be chosen to the inner circle of the school in relation to the scholarship of the Dark Arts.

Penny was quickly rummaging through items left by the late Roberta Smithers. Roberta had been one of the Science teachers and had worked at the school for over ten years. Unfortunately, she had recently passed away from a sudden heart attack, and her funeral was going to be down south in England. Roberta had been a spinster, so the school hadn't been sure who to send her personal belongings to, at first.

However, Penny noticed Roberta had been receiving letters for over a year now. She had seen one left in the staff room. By the look of the envelope, it had been handwritten. She remembered being intrigued.

1. She was surprised Roberta was getting any correspondence.
2. Who would be interested in her? She was so boring as a person.
3. Who still sent handwritten correspondence. Everything is either emails or texts, these days.

There wasn't anyone around, so she took out the already opened correspondence and read the letter. Curious who the mystery person might be. It wasn't long before she realised the mystery person wasn't a stranger after all. She knew her.........Daisy Redmond. She quickly put the letter back in its envelope and placed it back where she had found it.

***

Daisy had been in school together with Penny when they were younger and had been friendly enough. But had drifted apart as most do, when they are destined to go down different pathways in life. Penny's career had brought her to become the Head of this school. Which had always been her desire as she had family connections to it. Daisy on the other hand was quite content to become an English teacher, watchful. Always watchful but often annoyingly interfering as Penny recalled. She recalled Daisy had given it all up for some family issue and had moved back down to England. So why has Daisy been writing to Roberta?

***

Penny was in what had once been Roberta's bedroom and was looking around. She could see one of the staff had already started to box up some of her personal items as they were sitting on her bed. Whilst she was looking, she saw several letters put together and in turning them over, noticed they were written and in the same handwriting.

***

She took them and once in the safety of her office, read them one by one. She had been right about Roberta being no good. Why else would she have been in contact with Daisy. She didn't feel so bad about Roberta's demise when she realised it had been Roberta who had kept the precious emerald stone away from her. She would have been too weak to have done this on her own. But now she knew she'd been in touch with Daisy, it made more sense. With this knowledge, she didn't feel so bad about poisoning Roberta with an untraceable poison. The Medics had put it down to a heart attack.

'*Daisy, Daisy, you always were a thorn in my side. You were always the "little miss goody-two shoes".*' She had wondered where the stone had gone. Using her magic, she thought it would be easy to find, but alas it seemed Roberta had been one step ahead and must have put a protective spell on it, to protect its whereabouts. But now she was dead, the spell had died with her.

'*So why can't I find it?*' She thought. '*What if she's sent it somewhere for safe keeping?*'

Penny huffed out of her office and caught sight of Ms. Armitage the school's secretary, 'Jennifer! Where are you sending Roberta's personal belongings to?' Fake smile.

'She'd requested most of it go to Charity, but I believe there was something which she wanted to be forwarded on to a friend, down south. Do you want me to get the address for you? I also have the details of where her funeral is going to take place this coming Friday.' Ms. Armitage replied.

'If you could be a poppet and email me the address and where the funeral is taking place. I've had a change of heart. I will travel down and pay my respects to whoever shows up. I wasn't aware she had any family, but I guessed there must be someone.' Penny needed to be certain where the emerald stone had gone. She might have sent it to a distant relative. '*If that was the case*' Penny thought, '*I should be able to track it, as they'd be unaware of the importance of the stone. It would just be a trinket of sentimental value. But to those in the dark arts, it was a key to another dimension.'*

The next day Penny took the train down to Kings Cross station, in London. She'd booked in at a hotel, not far and enjoyed the Gothic architecture of the building reminding her of her school.

At the funeral, she blended into the background and waited until she was able to work out who were relatives and who might be old friends. She hoped she might see Daisy paying her respects to her old friend. After the service, she was gracious enough to talk with a few people who had known Roberta when she was younger.

***

Fortune was smiling down at her, as one had let slip Daisy had been expected to come to the funeral, but her health was faltering, and she was in the midst of Alzheimer's. She had come away with not only an interesting update on Daisy's health, but also given the address of her new care home which she was moving to.

Penny decided to stay a few days longer in London and whilst she was in her hotel room, she started a ritual to try and tap into the spirit of Daisy. It was a long shot, but it had been known that whilst a person was in a confused state, you could tap into their subconscious. She had no other choice after none of Roberta's relatives seemed to know anything about the precious stone. As she was about to close the ritual defeated, she got a glimpse of Daisy and tried to speak with her via telepathy. She got the sense that Daisy had recognised her for a moment, then she was gone.

'Well, well, well, Daisy how the mighty has fallen' she said mockingly. 'Fear not, my old friend, I will come and visit you soon'.

Two days later, she turned up at the home after having spoken to the receptionist. She'd given her some cock and bull story about her looking up her old friend. She came to the reception area and was speaking with Jenny, but Daisy had been quite upset getting settled in on that day. So, Penny had to leave, but not before leaving her business card.

'Ms. Penny S Quigley' the receptionist had read 'what does the S stand for? Sarah? Samantha?'

'No dear, it's Sylvana'

'What an unusual name, what does it mean'

'It's a very old family name, it means 'of the forest'' Penny replied with a smirk on her face. 'Please make sure you give Daisy my card, I'll be in touch' she said before turning 'one way or another' then continued walking away … she'd be back.

Witches Aren't Real

by Nicola Warner

Witches aren't real - that's what I was told. Just a myth - a fantasy, but that doesn't explain what I just witnessed. This woman didn't resemble the stereotype you see in story books. Her skin was not an "I'm about to puke" green, but a soft glow of bronze. She glittered under the artificial lights and was definitely a fan of Body Glow bronzer. She didn't fashion robes, nor a pointy hat, she was dressed in wide legged trousers and a finely knitted jumper. The only thing that I found odd was the fact that everything she wore was a rich green, perfectly matched, except her boots which I'm sure I've seen displayed in the window of River Island. She stood over the lifeless slump on the ground with a triumphant expression gliding across her face.

"At last!" she hissed as she wrapped a perfectly matched buttoned poncho around her shoulders.

Where the hell did that came from? I whispered to myself, as I stared with my mouth wide open. My brain churned over trying to make sense of it. '*Maybe she was already holding it?'* it suggested. *Well, it Could have been possible, I suppose it could have blended in and I'd just not noticed*, I replied with a sigh, a little disappointed with what my brain had conjured.

I watched as the Emerald silhouette moved across the verge in elegant strides without a return glace to what she had left curled on the ground. The bottom of her poncho surfed over the gentle breeze before disappearing completely, leaving nothing but a twinkle of smoke.

Witches Don't Exist

by Nicola Warner

10pm could not have struck sooner, this shift was as slow to start as it was to finish. Mr Kettering, widowed for 3 years, came to have his dinner the same time each night, he and his late wife would come here often, and he wanted to keep that connection. He usually ordered the same thing, but tonight, he changed his mind 3 times, before deciding on his usual beer-battered cod and chips. A young couple complained that their meal was not how they requested but decided a free desert would make up for their disappointment. The Assistant Manager sent her on dish duty half hour before closing, which she didn't mind doing, she just wished she had been appointed head dishwasher a little earlier in the evening, as it meant now she couldn't leave until the Kitchen was tidy, and Head Chef Peter Simms was not the tidiest cook.

As she left the restaurant side exit, she pulled her coat round her just a little tighter, almost giving herself a reassuring hug. She took a deep breath taking in the sharp British evening, she sighed. She made her way to her car, which was parked in the staff spaces closer to the building, but she would still panic run down the poorly lit ally towards the safety of her car.

She had tossed and turned most of the night. She finally managed to settle just as that rather annoying jingle from her phone disturbed her. She glared at the chest of drawers which her phone was dancing around on. Her enthusiasm was non-existent today. The thought of getting up, getting showered and dressed, was one step closer to leaving for the station. She felt a flush of guilt. It's not that she didn't want to see her aunt, it just made her sad to see her so confused and frustrated with herself. She felt helpless that there was nothing that she could do. '*Yes, there is!*' She told herself, '*You can get your backside up out of this bed and try to put a smile on your aunt's beautiful face! OK? GO!*' Feeling a rush of adrenaline after her pep talk, she freed herself from her duvet and made a charge for the bathroom.

Her aunt was diagnosed with Alzheimer's just over a year ago. Medication assisted in improving her concentration and memory; however, the effects were not as long lasting as they had hoped. She began to deteriorate quite quickly. It was stressful and it became apparent that it would be beneficial for her to move into a care home, where she would get the care she needed from people who specialised in dementia; and who knew what the hell they were doing.

Her Aunt was like a mother to her, she had raised her since she was 4 years old when her own mother had washed her hands of her, after deciding motherhood was just not for her. Her Aunt was more than happy to take on that role and beamed with pride, which shone brighter with each passing year. She always went above and beyond, nothing was ever too much. Her mother dipped into her life now and again, if she needed money, or a place to crash for the night.

The train station was dark and gloomy. The morning breeze still clung on to the chill from the night, the hanging baskets that decorated the station walls were dripping with morning dew. She hurried over to the ticket machine to avoid any awkward conversations with the grumpy looking man at the kiosk. She quickly made her way to the opposite platform to board the ready and waiting train.

She chose the quieter end of the train and took a seat by the window. It was a long journey ahead of her with multiple stops on the way. She placed her bag beside her to discourage any lonely passengers taking the empty seat as an invitation to tell her their life story. *Not today.*

She stared out of the window as the train pulled away thinking about nothing but her aunt, her mind wondering back to the appointment she attended with her last year. It was hard to tell who was more nervous about the results of the blood tests and brain scan. When the words Alzheimer's disease were mouthed by the consultant, white noise filled the room. Tears streamed down her aunt's face. It was clear that she did not quite understand … what was happening. She was getting more confused. The consultant was explaining a list of options for her … they can give her medication … cholinesterase inhibitors to help with her episodes of confusion. She squeezed her aunt's hand so tight, never wanting to let go.

The announcement of the next station bellowed through the carriage. This was her stop. She was thankful that the care home was just a short walk from the station. She did not feel comfortable getting into a taxi with a stranger in a different town. They always ask so many questions.

She stepped hesitantly towards the double glass doors; her heart thumped so hard it made her lightheaded. She paused to catch her breath before tottering through the reception area. She was greeted by an overexcited blonde at the front desk.

"Hello …" she squinted at the woman's name tag, "…Jenny," she smiled, "My aunt was, well she's more like a mother really, she was brought here as a new resident last week … my aunt's name is Daisy Redmond … I'm Esme Redmond … I have been speaking with someone over the phone, so you should be expecting me."

Jenny smiled politely, "Ah, Miss Redmond, of course, it's lovely to put a face to a name. Your aunt has been asking after you. Like I said before she's settled in so well. I'll take you down to her room. This way."

She followed Jenny down the hallway to room 9. She opened the door and happily announced her arrival, "Ms. Redmond, Esme is here to see you."

She walked through the door Jenny was holding open, and looked round the room, which resembled a small apartment. There was tea making facilities along the far wall, with a small dining table and chair either side. Her aunt was sat drinking a cup of tea, engrossed in the television. She stopped as the cup reached her lips and then carefully set it back down again. Her face lit up with a big smile and gestured Esme to sit in the vacant chair.

"Esme, darling, where have you been? I've been worried"

"I'm so sorry I couldn't come down with you last week, they put me down for a double shift, I tried to get out of it."

Her aunt waved her arms dismissively, "never mind that, darling. Have you seen Sylvana?"

"Who?" she frowned, "I don't think I know a Sylvana, do you?"

"Yes, I know Sylvana, you can't trust anything that

woman says. Promise me! Don't let her take it."

"Who is Sylvana? Take what?"

"When I was a girl, your grandmother told me about her. I was given precious gift. She said she was going to help me … show me how to use it. I need you to know… there will be people around to help you when I can't, but Sylvana is not one of them. Promise me!"

"Okay, I promise … I won't trust … Sylvana…"

"Good, I'm glad, shall we make tea?" Daisy made her way over to her little corner kitchen to put on the kettle.

"Aunt Daisy? Will you tell me who Sylvana is?"

"Sylvana? Goodness, where did you hear that name? I've not seen her in years. She's a witch."

Esme sat a little bewildered, she expected her aunt to be a little random with her conversations, but this had taken her by surprise. Who was Sylvana? Why shouldn't she trust her. Of course, her aunt didn't mean Sylvana was a real witch … did she? When she was younger her aunt would tell marvelous stories of all things witchy, but they were just stories … weren't they? Witches don't exist … right?

Her aunt placed a cup in front of her, "drink, up love, nothing worse than a cold brew."

The Gift

by Nicola Warner

Esme sat mesmerised by the swirling steam floating out of her cup.

"Is there something troubling you dear?"

Esme looked at her aunt and smiled in a bleak attempt to disguise her confusion. "I'm fine Aunt Daisy, sorry, just a little tired."

"Biscuit?" Daisy suggested, "biscuits always put a smile on your face when you were little, I'll get them."

"No, I'll get them, you sit and enjoy your tea."

Esme made her way over to the sideboard and pulled off the lid to a small Tupperware box, as she set the lid down, she noticed a small card on top of her aunt's post. It was a business card.

"Ms Penny S Quigley" she read, a little too loudly.

"What was that dear?"

"Um ... ooh custard creams!" Esme smiled as she made her way back to her seat and placed the box on the table.

Daisy smiled, "they were your favourite, but what a mess you would make with them," she shook her head at the fond memory.

Esme smiled behind the biscuit she helped herself to and glanced back over to the sideboard.

"What's troubling you, you look worried?"

"I'm fine aunt Daisy, honestly," she faked a smile.

"I may be losing my marbles, but I'm not blind, nor stupid. What's wrong?"

Esme sighed, "Did you get anything odd in your post this morning?"

"Nothing alarming, but in all honesty, I haven't looked yet, its normally just a load of leaflets, they go straight in the bin. Although I often get a lovely letter from a friend, you remember Roberta, don't you? I like writing to her, it gives me something to do here, and gives me something to look forward to, except for your visits, of course."

Esme's mouth fell open, dropping a few crumbs on the table, which made Daisy smile, " Aunt Daisy ... Roberta ... You do remember don't you ... she passed away ... you do remember don't you?"

"Oh goodness, oh yes ... of course I remember... oh how awful."

Esme studied her aunt's face, "are you ok Aunt Daisy?"

A breathless "yes" escaped her as she dabbed

around her eyes with a white cotton handkerchief, braving a smile she asked, "do you still have that locket I gave you for your thirteenth birthday?"

"Of course, I do."

***

Esme examined the perfectly wrapped rectangle. Her aunt urged her to open it, but Esme couldn't bring herself to, she would never be able to tie a bow like that.

"Goodness, you're the first child I have met who didn't want to open a present for fear of ruining the wrapping paper, I assure you, the magic is in the gift, not the wrapping."

Esme beamed, "it's just sooooo pretty! Can we take a photo first? Please?"

Daisy laughed, and grabbed the camera, "say cheese!"

Esme beamed at the camera and held her pose until the flash had faded from her eyes.

"Now will you open it?"

Esme nodded excitedly and pulled delicately at the end for the bow, which glided to the floor like an elegant feather. Underneath the sparkly wrapping was a red velvet box. Her aunt watched her eagerly, not wanting to miss the moment she saw it for the first time. Esme lifted open the box, her eyes widened. A golden locket suspended on a chain, it was round in shape with thin twisted bars, which wrapped around something sparkly like wild ivory. She investigated the golden cage, there was a deep glittering emerald still partly in its host rock dancing around loosely inside. It was enchanting. She had always had a fascination with crystals, but didn't have an emerald in her collection, and now she did.

Her fingers traced the delicate gold chain, "Wow!" she said finally.

"You should wear it everyday, dear! Its only safe when it is with you."

***

"You do keep it safe don't you?"

"Of course, I do," Esme smiled, "I keep it my jewelry box."

"Good, I'm glad you are keeping it safe, but it would be safer if you kept it on you."

"Is that your way of asking me to wear it more?" Esme laughed.

Daisy stared at her a little dazed, "yes, you do need to wear it more," she took a sip from her cup.

"Aunt Daisy? There's a business card over there, who is Penny Quigley?"

"Someone not to trust."

"Like Sylvanna?"

"They're one in the same." She took another sip of her tea.

"How did you get the card?"

"What card dear? Oh I've not forgotten your birthday have I?"

"No, Aunt Daisy, you haven't." Esme smiled, making a mental note to speak with Jenny before she leaves.

Nature

Nature Through Your Ages

by Tina Cooper

From the age of one-ish to about eight-ish everything is just amazing. Every. Single. Thing.

Trains, sand, toffee apples, socks, helping your mum cook, swings* and even a trip to the doctors can fill a wee soul with oooooh because everything is new and exciting but the thing that gets the young heart a fluttering more than anything is Mother Nature.

Bugs mainly but anything will do.

A simple leaf can be investigated for hours on end and a stick… Well, a stick can be anything you want it to be. A stick can be a horse, a witches broom, a gun, a lightsaber, a thing to point at other things with and, on the odd occasion, something to whack a sibling with.

Take your five-year-old to the woods and you'll have a wonderful time, no really. Remember, everything is amazing.

To be honest you don't really need to go to the woods.

When my daughter was small, we would lay on the decking in the garden and watch the tiny bugs forever. The decking sat above a small water feature installed by the previous owner so there was allsorts down there from miniature snails to spiders to frogs and multi-coloured caterpillars. We'd make a morning of it and take drinks and snacks.

Ahh, those truly were the days as she has since gone to the dark side or Xbox as it's more commonly known.

When we get to around nine or ten-ish our love of all things natural can wane a bit. We have discovered the television and movies, we are too cool for ladybirds and paddling in streams. We are with our mates doing matey type things like learning to swear and thinking we know everything.

At this point it is still possible to get your ten-year-old on their own and impress them with a sunrise or a meteor shower, just, but they are soooo over a caterpillar or a snail.

Soon, too soon, we hit our drunken teens and twenties.

Few people notice nature in their twenties because they are sozzled and only thinking about all things heart related. In my early twenties I didn't wear socks in the winter, or ever, can you imagine a life without socks? Such was my awareness of the changing seasons that I didn't notice the cold. I could queue outside a nightclub wearing very little even on the coldest of evenings because I was not fifty. At fifty you need socks as much as you need the air that you breathe.

Later, much later if you are slow to the parade like me, you will find love then suddenly and inexplicably decide that children would be nice. Children can be nice but don't be fooled, they can also suck the goodness out of your soul whilst magically making you love them more.

Children are evil geniuses.

But.

Children do love a miniature snail and will reignite in you a long-forgotten love of the simple things in life. For example, the jam sandwich. Why do jam sandwiches get forgotten? They're like a cake for one, they're brilliant.

Anyhow.

This renewed love of nature is a whole new affair in that when you are small you love the snail but when you have small children you love that they love the snail. The wonder in their grubby, usually sticky, little faces will fill your cold dead heart with all the joy you once had until you were old enough to drink in pubs.

Then, just as you're getting into the swing of things and you know your ladybug from your humbug, your children become bigger and less interested, so the bug investigations cease.

That's ok, you haven't the time anyway. Too busy washing, answering the thousands of daily emails from their schools and having small but perfectly formed panic attacks about how rubbish the world is whilst wondering if there's any point to anything ever.

Then, as your children need you less and lesserer, and you're too old to be a tipsy twenty-year-old dancing with a stranger in a dingy club, you begin to wonder about the snail.

How long do they live? How do snails make baby snails? If you say "hello little fella" can they hear you? Do they sleep?

Slowly but surely, you begin to notice the changing of the seasons, the colours of the leaves and you begin to like the feeling of the wind in your sails. You find it odd because you're on your own just looking in wonder at all the delightful things that have always been there. You enjoy rediscovering a crystal clear stream or listening to the birds. Suddenly the birds become loud yet oddly soothing.

You get a little cross with yourself because you know you once knew the names of the birds and the varieties of trees, but you replaced that knowledge with Calpol doses and number lines so now you only recognise herons and that's only because you are terrified of the prehistoric looking horrors. Herons shouldn't be that big!

Still, you like the sound of whatever bird it is, it's an ancient sound, one that humans have been hearing since Adam was stealing apples and will continue to hear long after you have moved on to wherever you believe you will move on to.

You will find yourself standing at the edge of a freshly ploughed field admiring how straight the lines are whilst pretending you don't know that those huge machines all run on satellite navigation now so will rarely create a wobbly groove.

Time will continue on, as she is wont to do, and you will realise that you now need to hear the birds and feel the wind and rain on your troubled face. Enjoying outside as you pass from inside to inside is one thing but going outside because you want to go outside brings with it a feeling of immense freedom.

To stop what you're doing and step outside, even for a few moments, reminds you that the world will keep turning with or without you and that you'd really rather it be with.

To stop when you really shouldn't is even better.

When you're in the middle of a dull conversation, excuse yourself, go outside and just breathe instead. When you're half way through a meeting, go outside and have a good sniff. When it's late and you've just remembered the uniforms need ironing, go outside and look up at the sky for a bit. When you should be cooking yet another unwanted dinner for your family, go outside and look for a snail or a particularly interesting twig or two.

Just go outside.

If in doubt, just nip out.

*you're never too old for the swings

On these long endless days
by Lewis Green

Extract from forthcoming novel

On these long endless days there is not much for her to do but to plot and ponder. Trudging along with aching limbs her memories come to her like sunshine through branches. Sometimes they leave as quickly as they arrive, like a bird just out of sight, that alights at the slightest noise. Birdsong at dawn, that stops just as soon as you open your eyes.

She remembers the day she left home, how she walked through the shell of that once happy place, leaving footprints in the ash.

She trod lightly through the rooms as if afraid of scaring away the ghosts of any memories that remained. She ran her hand along the mantel, leaving a swirl of dust and lint in its wake. She stooped to pick up a bent and broken picture frame. Four smiling faces. Sisters, mother, father. The glass cracked and covered in a fine layer of dust, except for the place where her father stared back. She remembers her mother at the kitchen table whispering to herself and cradling the frame, stroking the image of his face. The only thing left of him.

Her best days. She and her sister would wake early to watch their father saddle the horse. The breath plumed from its nostrils as he whispered to it and rubbed its snout. The girls were gathered in his greatcoat against the early morning frost. A blanket tucked around them as they tottered on the horse through the pale dawn light. Deer stared at the curious sight; this horse laden with a three-headed bundle. Rabbits dart to and fro in the hedges and stand on hind legs to watch them pass.

Through meadows he would name all the different trees and plants they passed. They stopped at streams to water the horse and fill the canteens, their father pointing out the berries that were safe to eat and those best avoided. Those to cure a rash and those to cause one. Those from which you could make tea.

The girls took off their boots and waded up to their knees, shrieking from the glassy cold against their legs. Their father leant against the horse smoking his pipe.
They sat on a log to dry their feet and ate sandwiches from the saddle bag. The girls took turns feeding the horse chunks of apple.

"Girls, don't tease him…here, come and look at this…"

From his pocket he took a crumpled piece of paper, folded into eight. The map he showed them was well worn and fraying along the folds, but unmistakably showed the place they currently inhabited.

He traced his finger along the bank of the stream and his finger carried with it a smudge of pencil lead.

"Look here…you see this space in the circle."

"Yes papa."

"It's right here, yonder."

They step over the log they are sitting on and head towards a spot shaded by a copse of trees a hundred yards from the stream.

"What's here Papa?"

"Our new home."

"But there's nothing here."

"Not yet there isn't…we have to build it first."

"What will we have?"

"What do you want? We'll have all this land."

"A cabin?"

"Uh huh, of course…we can have a stable and have space for more horses."

"Can we each have a horse Papa?"

"It depends…can you keep this a secret from your mother for a while?"

178

They both nod their heads in unison.

"Then you can both have a horse."

They lay for a while in the tall grass enjoying the sun on their faces and watching insects take flight. Their father fashions a bundle of small branches to use as firewood and ties it to the back of the saddle.

A rumble of thunder in the distance. Their father looks to the west.

"Let's get you home."

It is almost dark as they get home. A kiss for each of them as they reach the porch, as if they had been gone for days, not a matter of hours.

Their mother fusses over them, gives them sugary tea, bread, and butter. Her father produces a bundle from behind his back. "Happy birthday, little one."

From the bundle she takes a porcelain doll. Two shining black eyes, and blonde curly hair beneath a bonnet chequered peach and white.

Later their mother lights candles and pushes a log into the fire filling the room with a wavering orange light. The wind rattles in the stovepipe and they listen to the patter of rain on the windowpanes. The girl watches her father pensive in thought as he sits by the fire smoking his pipe. The flames flicker and throw a tangle of shadows across his face. Marionette, monster, cloud. The hours she spent watching him whittle sticks by the fire with his pocketknife. Hours never wasted. How he could forge beauty from nothingness. Miniature forest creatures hewn from the plainest piece of wood. Hours when he never spoke. Stopping only to wipe sweat from his brow or to fling shavings into the fire.

She pushes now at a pile of logs beneath the mantle with the toe of her boot. One stubborn log leans but doesn't topple. She picks it up and turns it. Protruding from the log is her father's pocketknife. She skewers it free and clasps it shut. Holding her breath, she stares at the knife in her palm as if she is seeing it for the first time.

She hesitates at the door, takes one last look around. She takes Pitseleh from her place on the shelf and wipes the dust from her face. The doll is cold to the touch.

Without looking back, she nestles Pitseleh in the crook of her arm and steps into the night.

Unwanted Guests

by Bob Bootman

We have a mouse, inside the house

Under the bathroom floor

Not very nice, it may be mice

There may be three of four

Put down some bait, I couldn't wait

For the mousetrap to arrive

On CCTV, I counted three

Then spotted another five

In a bit of a state, now that there's eight

Poison the only solution

Placed a menu, at each mouse venue

And planned their execution

Rodenticides, and more besides

Are put upon their 'table'

Some warfarin, to make blood thin

I wish I'd read the label

Don't know why, take days to die

After crawling back into bed

They start convulsing, which sounds repulsing

Before they end up dead

The mice disappeared; the family cheered

Our problems, they are not

Up our noses, no smell of roses

As bodies start to rot

A little mouse tomb, underneath our room

I should've been more clever

The odour of death, took away our breath

That smell will be with us forever

Obtuse

Hiding in Plain Sight

by Bob Bootman

Dripping with gold, in his golden tracksuit
Red tinted glasses and golden hair
Running marathons, raising money
If only
We were more aware
Of the monster behind the angel
Evil mind
Hiding in plain sight
Charitable saint during daytime
Predatory paedo at night

People knew
What he was doing
But decided not to tell
Could have protected vulnerable children
For whom it didn't end well

It was all swept under the carpet
Until shortly after he died
No justice for the victims
Who kept it concealed
While they cried

Pedicabo Ego Vos

by Bob Bootman

I sit at the head of the table

Prone to prevarication

I cannot seem to tell the truth

With total tergiversation

The catastrophe of covid

The reversing of the rules

The lateness of the lockdown

I keep fibbing to you fools

Terminological inexactitudes

Of every shape and size

Like a spider I am spinning

A deceitful web of lies

They call me Bullshit Boris

Jackass Johnson, all the same

No mistakes or misdemeanors

No, NOT ME, I'm NOT to blame

I am innocent, unimpeachable

Beyond reproach, I am the boss

You're all stuck with Bullshit Boris

Pedicabo ego vos

Playing With Words

Covid

by Tina Cooper

Cruel in ways we could never have imagined

Funerals without solace

Weddings without guests

We await our curve to be flattened

Our simplest pleasures supplanted

A chat with a stranger

A trip to the shop

Such small things but all taken for granted

Vaccination of the masses

Now the only way forward

All tired of isolation

And the constant sitting on our asses

Incredible they are to me

The masks and the gel

Distance now social

Two meters now the key

Days become months

The months everlasting

Time now somehow meaningless

In this, a global down in the dumps

Homophonic Tail

by Bob Bootman

Aisle tell ewe the tail of a very tall mail

Didn't bye his wife any flours

Wile honey-mooning in Niece

He kneeded sum piece

She'd bee board of hymn Inn ours

It started to reign, sew they flu on a plain

To Grease and I'm knot gonna lye

His efforts in vane

She was clearly in pane

Their four he eight humble pi

Fluores-Puss

by Bob Bootman

Big-whizzed and wazzled
Be-fuddled, be-dazzled
Contricious, delicious
Malevolent, malicious

Incredibly incredulous
The flaming Fluores-Puss
Exciting, inviting
Fizz-foaming and frightening

I found a flaw-mation
An intimidation
I gas-tanked and goaded
And then he exploded!

BANG!

Cat-astrophic combustion
Rainbow-onic eruption
Bright colours collectively boom
Feline fluorescence
Kitty effervescence
That cat decorated the room

The Gift of Poetry
by Bob Bootman

Buying Byron in a bookshop
Wanted 'Darkness' and 'Don Juan'
One was for my daughter
And the other for my son

Couldn't afford the both of them
Got a little bit upset
One child will be disappointed
And I began to fret

Took them to the till point
Tears welling in my eyes
Salesman smiled sweetly
I received a nice surprise

Only charged me for the 'Darkness'
'Don Juan', he gave to me
Special offer for the weekend
It was Byron, get 'Juan' free

Quickies

24-hour Fixation

by Bob Bootman

An interminable infatuation

Round-the-clock, I am contritely

Thinking about Tess Daly

And dreaming of Keira Knightley

Cats Eyes

by Bob Bootman

Don't give me that

You crafty cat

Why do you look

At me

Like that?

Can't be hungry

We both know

I fed you

Only

An hour ago

Congranulations

by Bob Bootman

I crushed the Colombian coffee beans

Waited while they percolated

Had brewed the perfect coffee

And for that, was congranulated.

Eyes

by Nicola Warner

His eyes held a thousand pictures

That could speak a thousand words

They witnessed all the heartache

And the sadness of the world

Still he Carried on

Whilst he lived in fear

He held his family close

Shedding a silent tear

Gangster's Revenge

by Bob Bootman

Gangsters crept into the house

Legends of drug dealing

Fraud the cause of losing cash

Discovered the accountant stealing

Revenge now came upon him

Splendid fires started

Essentially, he fried to death

Burned 'til he was departed

Inflation

by Martyn Kempson

Fifty years ago in Park Street, Luton

You could get the shit kicked out of you

If you looked twice at the wrong person.

Today a smart shop in the same street

charges fifty pounds for colonic irrigation.

Martyn Kempson Quickies

My cats touch noses

Softly in formal greeting

like maori warriors.

Is a tricycle

one and a half times better

than a bicycle?

Poem

by Tina Cooper

Tumble dryer fluff

Is fascinating stuff

Test of My Commitment

by Bob Bootman

I joined Weightwatchers online today

They posed a question, just for rookies

A pop-up appeared upon the screen

'Would you like to accept all cookies?"

Reflections

New Beginnings

by Tina Cooper

The writing prompt, from Creative Hats, this week is new beginnings. Not a problem, how hard can that be?

Very, as it happens. The thing is, there are so many of them.

Should I write about starting a new school, job or relationship? Starting a new piece of writing or a new piece of artwork? Surely starting anything is a beginning. To start is to begin. You could start building an extension or start a conversation. Both are new and also very much beginnings.

Oh dear. Too many to choose from.

Wait… endings are also new beginnings…

A divorce is a new beginning. Leaving school, leaving your teens or getting fired from your job. All are new beginnings and now my head hurts. Is that a beginning? Well yes, I'm beginning to need paracetamol.

In fact, there cannot be a beginning without an ending.

Perhaps it's not paracetamol that I need, it might be a drink.

pours herself a stiff one

When I got married I began my new life as a wife at the exact same time as my single life ended. I know, it was a surprise to me too. No transition period, no opportunity to enjoy a taster marriage to see if I liked it, just an instant switch from not married to very married.

Giving birth is one of the most significant beginnings I've ever experienced but it was also an ending. Suddenly I was a new, fairly incompetent, mother of an actual human but I had also ceased being a person who wasn't responsible for an actual human. Even my second foray into motherhood was the end of my being a mother of one. Gemma, our fellow writer, has just become a mother of three and ceased life as a mother of two. Why would she do this? Love and lunacy combined is the only explanation.

When I began my new enterprise, stay at home mum, it was the end of my life as a postie. When the postie life ended there was a new beginning.

Am I just wandering around in circles now?

Beginning. Ending. Beginning. Ending. Repeat.

When today began, yesterday ended.

When breakfast ended, the wait for lunch began.

When the lockdown began, our freedom ended.

When the lockdown ended, our anxiety began.

When the washing machine began to spin, our wearing of dirty clothes had ended.

When my dad's life ended, mum's widowhood began.

When autumn began, summer ended.

And so on and so on…

So, there it is, as clear as the day is lengthy.

Beginnings are endings or something equally profound.

pours herself another stiff one followed by another and another until a woozy booze induced sleep begins that also ends the awakeness

Personal reflection prompts …
by Tina Cooper

Do You Like Being Alone?
Yes. I love being alone but I wouldn't want to do it permanently. I like people very much, those I already know and those I'm yet to meet.

Do You Have a Hard Time Making Decisions?
Oh dear, yes, I cannot make a decision, I'm so bad I don't much like making decisions for my kids. It's their life to do with as they please but they are bonkers so I have to step in sometimes.

How Well Do Rewards and Incentives Work to Motivate You?
They don't but give me a deadline and I'm on it. That said, if you were to offer me food for a job well done...

Under What Conditions Do You Do Your Best Work?
When there's nobody about, the washing machine and dishwasher are doing their thing and the dog has been out. Then and only then I can justify sitting down to write.

Do You Hold Grudges?
Yes and no. I hold two grudges. One with an old boss and the other with the teacher that manhandled my son when he was five. If I see her my blood begins to boil. Other than that, I generally forget whatever it is I have the hump about pretty quickly. I haven't the memory space to stay cross.

Do You Take More Risks When You Are Around Your Friends?

Hahaha, no.

Do You Apologize Too Much?

Funnily enough I am trying to cut down, doctors orders.

What Animal Are You Most Like?

Just asked The Husband, he said the sloth.

How Good Is Your Sense of Direction?

Terrible. I still get lost at Swiss Gardens and I've worked there for almost 5 years. This Saturday will be my first day of lone working so, if I don't turn up next week, come and get me.

What Assumptions Do People Make About You?

That I am unsociable because I don't always jump at an invite. You can tell as many people as you like that you have me/cfs they'll still assume you're just lazy or grumpy or both. For the record I'm neither. Well, not every day.

Apparently, I'm hard to get to know, I've been told this more than once, and folks wonder what goes on inside my head. Not much to be honest but don't tell anyone, I prefer folks to think I'm mysterious.

A friend once told me that she admired me from afar, before our kids landed at the same school, and all because of my boots. So, people assume I have excellent taste in boots. This is the very friend who pushed me to come to college. I love her dearly; she is very wise.

Writing

by Tina Cooper

I wonder why we do it? Write that is?

Manuals I understand, how to change a tyre on your car or the bag in your hoover. Instruction manuals are, mostly, necessary, and rather handy.

Guidebooks, oh how I love thee. I buy a guidebook wherever I go then pop them with all my other guidebooks never to see the light of day again. I imagine that I will return to a place and will be ready, guidebook in hand. This has yet to be the case. Usually, I forget having bought a guidebook and will merrily buy another resulting in two unread guidebooks. I am undeterred in my purchasings though. Still cannot pass a guidebook.

Stories are a no brainer. Everyone loves a good story, young and old. From Milo and his tollbooth to that fella at Bates Motel or anything written by Stephen Fry, we all love a good story. I say good because there are some terrible ones out there hiding among their betters waiting to waste your time, time you could have spent cutting your nails or staring into space.

The thing is, I do none of the above.

I have never written a handy manual or an informative guidebook* and, try as I might, I cannot locate my imagination, so a story is yet to emerge from the draughty corners of my nonsense filled noggin. This all leaves me with very little to say for myself.

This doesn't stop me though. It should but it doesn't.

*My mum says I should write a public toilet guidebook as I cannot pass one without entering, one day perhaps.

Shorts

Autumn Evening Confusion

By Paul Clark

As I walked to the perimeter gate

For a moment I thought about fate

The recycling bin was in dark shade

My nerves were so frayed

Whistling men if Harlech

That bin, in shadow, it was a Dalek

Now, I am an old bin survivor

Lucky then, sonic screwdriver

I should have blinked

Black cat on fence just winked

I blinked back so very wide

To recover, a pint of Broadside!

A Wet Wednesday in Whitehall

by Martyn Kempson

A public space but fenced off,

and shunned by tourists,

trees, shrubs and grass united in neglect.

Scattered statues, shiny wet,

testifying to the deeds of long dead marshals.

They serve as roundabouts for endless jogger streams

while workers and homeless discreetly space themselves

on benches with their drug of choice.

Here are the warlords who held the line in pointless
sacrifice.

And here is Samuel Plimsoll who drew the line for the
drowned soldiers.

Foot

by Tina Cooper

I've hurt my foot

I don't know how

It was ok

But it's not now

I've walked the dog

And all was well

My foot was fine

Sound as a bell

I popped on a shoe

And felt a twinge

I did not whine

I did not winge

I carried on

Some courage I plucked

The problem is

My foot is now really really sore

Give me a Break

by Bob Bootman

Holidays should be my get-away

From the stresses and strains of work

But my colleagues still try to find me

Which can really get me irked

In France, they try to phone me

In Texas, sending texts

In Egypt, showered with emails

Not sure where I'm going next?

Why do I have to be disturbed?

By email, text and phone?

Book a break in Communicado

Pigs on Course

by Paul Clark

Two pigs thought to spend the day

On the local fair, fairway

Golfers to scare and chew

And roll around in the morning dew

Lightcliffe, Halifax was great venue

To entertain the porcine two

They came back for a second day

The Tuesday after Sabbath day

They returned to nudge flags

And try clubs and bags

At the moment it's calm

The sequel to Animal Farm?

Travels

Beside Myself

By Tina Cooper

Some moons ago, before the kids arrived with the storks when we had money and energy and a zest for travel, The Husband and I booked a trip to Crete.

I've not been abroad for a while now but back then it was customary to attend a meeting at the hotel where a too jolly holiday rep would regale you with tales of day trips and tell you where the nearest doctor could be found.

We booked Knossos, obviously, and a day trip to Egypt.

Egypt? Me, in Egypt? Surely not. Other people get to go to Egypt, not little old me from Bedfordshire in England.

We left at midnight on a dornier jet, whatever that is, and without any luggage. That was an odd sensation, to board with only a rucksack, I liked it very much. The plane was rather posh, so posh that we were given a glass of something fizzy. No idea what it was but I was already feeling special so I supped the fizz with an air of celebrity.

Once the sun came up I could see out of the window and everything was brown, the buildings, roads and even what I think were fields were brown.

When we landed we were greeted by cheery staff who popped flowery garlands around our necks. I could have cried.

I was beside myself.

I had arrived in Egypt, a country I had never thought I'd travel to, a country not for the likes of me. It felt like the adventure it so clearly was.

At the coach, our transport for the day, we were given an armed guard and two police escorts. Weirdly I thought nothing of this, still too excited, and settled down for a small but perfectly formed excitement weep. Not sure if I've mentioned it but I was about to burst from the sheer madness of it all.

I was in Egypt for goodness sake!

EGYPT!

We drove through the City Of The Dead where I spotted a man on a moped with a goat attached then on we went to the pyramids.

We were allowed in one of the pyramids, the pyramid of Khafre I think. I didn't like it much and was relieved to see daylight again. Someone told me later that they were stuck in there during a power cut. No. Just no. We had our photo taken by two armed guards who then asked for money, something we would have to get used to it seemed.

Onwards to a very swanky hotel with a waterfall in the foyer where we ate something forgettable before heading to the Cairo Museum to see Tutankhamun's mask. It was bigger than I expected. I looked directly at it only to be told never to look directly at it.

Next stop was a papyrus shop where you could watch the making of the papyrus and buy one with your name on it. Obviously, we bought a papyrus with our names painted on it, it is a thing of beauty despite our names being spelled T I N A and B A L L.

As if this wasn't enough excitement for one day we then went on a cruise along the Nile where we watched two lovely ladies dance in colourful swirly skirts and ate cold chips.

But the highlight for me was the bazaar.

By then it was dark, the bazaar was beautifully lit and it hummed with the voices of the stall holders. I felt it all. I could feel the sounds and the smells as though they were reaching out to touch only me. It sounds lame but it was truly magical… for me at least.

Before we left the coach, we were told not to take any money, only a little loose change, no cameras, no jewellery and no jackets or easy to remove clothing.

I did not care; I was an overexcited moth to the flame.

The Husband on the other hand…

Apparently, unlike myself, he was aware of our surroundings, he could see that I was being eyed up by all and sundry because I looked as gullible as a gullible thing.

My eyes were out on stalks, my mouth wide in a grin to rival that of the Cheshire cat and my guard was very much switched off.

The most beautiful child I have ever seen planted herself

in front of me and pinned a small butterfly brooch to my t-shirt.

"One euro," she said.

I took the brooch off and gave it back to her. I didn't have any money, the few coins I'd taken with me I had spent on a miniature carved scarab. I now wonder where that is. I keep everything so it can't have gone far.

The stunning ten, maybe eleven, year old proceeded to pop the brooch back on to my t-shirt.

"One euro," she smiled.

This tooing and froing continued for quite some time.

To be honest, had I had any money on me, I would have given her everything, her eyes were hypnotic and glorious. I loved her instantly.

Back on the coach The Husband confessed to being nervous. I was surprised, he's never nervous, that and because I hadn't noticed the danger of the day. The need for an armed guard and a police escort should have been a bit of a giveaway but I was blind to it all.

I had spent the entire day bubbling with excitement. Not a single second had been lost to me, I was buzzing continuously for twenty-four hours straight.

Fast forward to last Wednesday.

Last Wednesday passed without the need for an armed guard, a police escort and without anyone asking me for one euro but it did have a similar fit to burst level of "oh my god, I can't believe I'm here."

Last Wednesday I was at Harry Potter Land.

I was beside myself again.

Bike

by Martyn Kempson

Each day hard on four

she cycles slowly past my door

with a rusty rattle and mouse like squeak

as old bones and oily chain creak

she rides a sit up beg machine.

Going somewhere or just been?

Storm trooper helmeted fighting the weather

scarfed, gloved and buttoned together

two miles an hour is her grim advance.

Another world from the Tour de France.

Lost and out of 'Lack'

by Bob Bootman

T'was a Monday when they found him

His clothes were old and smelly

His beard had grown quite long and grey

Trailed down just past his belly

He'd been lost for over seven years

Separated from his friend

His family thought that he was dead

No-one could comprehend

The journey he had taken

Over seven thousand miles

Just walking round in circles

Through Ikea's furniture aisles

He'd started off in 'Kallax'

Then got a glimpse of 'Lack'

He had followed all the arrows

But then he doubled back

Got lost between 'Kleppstad' and 'Malm'
Turned left at 'Baggebo'
Found a short cut to 'Gronlid'
But a sign there told him "No!"

Survived on Swedish meatballs
And drinking 'Dryck Blabar'
Each time he went to exit
He didn't get very far

Would fall asleep on a sofa
Sometimes eight hours, or more
By the time that he had woken up
They'd gone and shut the store

Each day would be the same for him
He'd try to find the way
But he'd end up back at 'Kallax'
It was just like Groundhog Day

He almost gave up trying

Time to accept his fate

Seven years inside Ikea

Didn't want to make it eight

Then that Monday afternoon arrived

On a 'Slattum' he was spread

It was then his brother spotted him

He'd come to buy a bed

Was ecstatic that they found him

Round his neck their arms were flung

And then he told his story

In a fluent Swedish tongue

New Beginnings

by Lewis Green

Extract from forthcoming novel

They walked that night through woods, wild and all encompassing, watched from heights and all around by owls and other nocturnal eyes. The tree roots they passed were steeped in a copper colour that ran off into streams like rust deposits from ships abandoned long ago. The cold rattled in their teeth and they stamped their boots on the snow, which lay atop red clay that, like an ancient horror buried beneath tried to reveal itself with every unsteady trip or step. The wind making their cloaks bulge and writhe like living creatures.

This strange caravan of migratory labourers blow into their hands for warmth. A bedraggled group of around forty, with hands buried in pockets and scarves pulled tight over faces are under the protection of Timms and his men, as they squint their eyes against the snow and press on into the bitter cold of the night.

Three horse-pulled wagons lead the way, filled with tents, tarps, clothes, sacks of kindling, and canned provisions enough to last at least until they reach the next settlement maybe two long days away. Each wagon emblazoned in white paint with *Blue Ridge Trail Co.*

Lanterns swinging at eye level, illuminate their path as a man in a top hat and redingote, taller by a head than the rest, calls the party to a halt before stepping to the tree line where he places his lantern on the ground and steps into the darkness, his figure slowly diminishing from view as he moves to the interior, fading the further he goes, stepping from shadow into darker shadow. After a while he emerges, spits in his hands and rubs them together. Picking up his lantern, he whistles before falling in line again behind the last wagon.

A motley crew, grime-smeared and gap-toothed all. Some of the men have more fingers than teeth. Some do not. This is no place for the girl. She follows closely behind. Her high cheek bones and slender nose lay beneath a fine layer of dirt. No more than fourteen, the girl far too young to be on this trail, with these people, none her kin. Her hair is blonde and shoulder-length, parted in the middle and tied together loosely at the back in a single, simple knot. Her boots bear water marks from where she has stood too long in the snow. Beneath her arm she carries a doll, hair straggly and limp beneath its bonnet. The snowfall stings her eyes, and collects on the shoulders of her coat as the party pushes further into the blizzard.

Maria, Timms' wife, stays close to the girl. Seeing the girl's hair fall around her face in loose strands, Maria takes it upon herself to fix it for her. She ties a coil that rests on top of the girl's head – in the French style. Maria knows nothing of the girl who she has only known for two weeks, when the party left out of Tennessee – nor why she has a fixed stare on her face, nor why she hasn't said a single word in those two weeks past. Maria, with hair pins in the mouth, hums as she works at the hair. She speaks continuously to the girl, knowing full well she won't get a reply. Maria doesn't care. Maria never had a daughter.

Some of the party stagger under the effort of another long day's walking. A Dutchman slips to his knees and is quickly helped to his feet by his friends. A broad-shouldered man steps out of the convoy and approaches the man in the top hat.

"Arthur, let us make camp here."

"Not yet, we'll stop yonder...we need to get through this next stretch...it's not safe here."

"Arthur, be reasonable...everyone is tired, they're dead on their feet."

"Do they pay us to get them there alive or get them there rested?"

"Yea, but still..."

"Listen Corsair, I pay you for your skill with a rifle, not your womanly compassion."

The man named Corsair trudges back to his place in the convoy, muttering to no-one in particular as he falls back in step with the others "...stubborn as a mule son of a bitch..."

Timms felt his shame rise. "Hold up here a minute damn ye." Timms left the trail and walked into the woods. He planted himself on a tree half uprooted by a recent storm and knocked his pipe against his boot to empty it. He thumbed tobacco into the pipe and tamped it down, all the while muttering under his breath "Goddamn Corsair...son of a doxy's purse."

Arthur Timms never wanted to be a hard-nosed chief. He never wanted to be a chief at all, and fell into it quite by accident. As he sat brooding on his upturned tree trunk he recalled the bizarre turn of events that led him to this current chapter of his life.

Twelve years prior, Timms was taken on as an apprentice by a man named Daniel Laurie. Laurie's *Blue Ridge Trading Co.* had been hired to transport two wagons of supplies to a small trading outpost ten miles east over a pass between the Alleghenies.

Laurie's daughter Maria watched as the young apprentices struggled under the weight of the supplies. She checked the horse's shoes and led them to the water troughs, before packing a sack of oats into the rear wagon, whilst the men continued loading supplies. Before they set off they ate beef stew round a large table pushed hastily against the side of the stable. Maria went to and from the scullery, keeping bowls topped up and bread buttered. Her mother brought fresh loaves from the kitchen and cups of warm beer for each man. The apprentices drank eagerly and the one called Arthur spilt his cup in his lap. Maria stifled a laugh and passed him a dishcloth. She thought him simple-minded. After she had cleared the dishes from the table, she kissed her father goodbye. She would see him in two days on his return.

They'd started out at dusk in a flurry of snow. Laurie marked their route on a roughly drawn map, waving a cigar at a yet unseen point in the distance. They passed The Shepherds Rest tavern on the edge of the outpost and Timms shivered at the creak of the sign in the wind. An icy shiver up his spine. To this day he can remember the creak of the sign in the wind. Timms brought up the rear of the convoy – he carried a rifle over his shoulder and led a gray mare by the reins. They picked their way through the mountains, each with a lantern to cut the dark, their breath coming ragged and heavy. Apart from the crunch of their boots on the snow and the snorting of the horses, it was silent. After three miles they stopped to catch their breath and to rest the horses. While they rested, Laurie plotted a new route with his cigar, the furnace-glow as he took a drag, illuminating his face for a brief moment before dissolving into darkness once more. Timms watched Laurie's cigar trace an arc in the sky and disappear forever. As they stood up to move, Laurie cracked his whip to get them moving again. In slow motion the snow gave way in front of them, sending men, horses, and wagons into the infinite blackness below. Timms froze as he watched them fall through the air. They didn't even have time to make a sound. He couldn't comprehend the silence that came next. They were simply there. And then they weren't. He stood where he was for what seemed like hours, staring into the darkness beyond, not daring even to breathe out. Evangeline *plumed her breath over his shoulder and trampled from side to side. "Easy girl...easy does it." He walked the horse backwards onto a solid bank of shale and rubbed her snout. Her breath plumed hot and moist against his face. "Well girl, that's not something you see every day."*

From the scullery window, Maria watched the young apprentice walk back into the stable with Evangeline. She thought it strange that he was alone and thought perhaps her father had sent him back to collect something they'd forgotten. When he hadn't come out from the stable after twenty minutes, she took up a lantern hanging on a hook outside the scullery door and headed for the stable.

The snow was coming down harder now and she couldn't see more than a few yards in front of her, despite the lantern's glow.

"Hello...hello, Arthur?"

There was no answer so she swung the stable door inwards and peered inside. There was no-one to be seen, but Evangeline whinnied in her stall at the far end of the stable.

"Hello...Arthur...are you in here?"

She brought the lantern up to her eyes and stepped forward into the gloom. She edged along the stable slowly towards Evangeline's stall.

"Arthur, this isn't funny..."

As she approached the stall she stroked the horse and removed the reins. "Hey girl...where is everyone?"

From the darkness at the back of the stall came a muffled moan. She peered into the darkness and gasped.

She found Arthur Timms wrapped in a bundle of blankets asleep on the floor of the stall with the horse.

She tended to him for the next two days, days in which he didn't move from his bundle of blankets. He mumbled to himself as if a fever held him, but she could make no sense of what he was saying. She fetched him food from the kitchen and brought him clean blankets. On the third day, she took Evangeline for a slow walk along the paddock and was surprised to see Arthur following behind still wrapped in his cosy shroud of blankets. Although she had guessed by now that her father wasn't coming home, she listened patiently as Arthur Timms told his story. How they staggered their way through the mountains. How the blizzard froze their beards and eyelashes. How they faced-off a mountain lion. How they laughed when Billy Grady pissed in his trousers when he saw it. How the dark bowl of the night sky expanded infinitely before them the higher they rose. How the thing he remembers the most when he closes his eyes is the silence before the fall. The glow of their cigars in the dark. The creak of the sign. The creak of the sign in the wind.

***

As sure as October would turn to November, so autumn would turn to winter. Snow covered the trees in long white tendrils. A cross was fashioned and the crossbeam tied with string dyed purple. Maria's mother would come early every morning to stand in front of the grave that would never hold a body and stare wild-eyed at the mountains to the east.

She and Maria liked having the young apprentice around the place – something about him reminded them of what they had lost – his unassuming presence, his stooping frame, his gentleness with the horses, the way Evangeline followed him everywhere. By and by, Maria would find excuses to bump into him around the homestead and found herself blushing whenever he was near. She started wearing her hair in different ways, her mother noted, smiling to herself. On Sundays they would ride out together and spend the day fishing. Arthur taught her to gut and clean the fish. She admired the savagery in the way he wiped the blade across his trousers to clean it. A simple man for simple times, she thought.

They were married in the spring, beneath an oak tree strung with ribbons. Becoming a husband commenced a new chapter in Arthur's life and brought to a close his period of mourning for the

229

men lost in the mountains. Maria wore her mother's yellow dress and had flowers woven into her hair. A crown of daisies. Arthur wore a navy shirt buttoned to the neck. He shook as he read his vow. That night he held her face in his hands and watched her sleep. It would be hours before he would fall to sleep himself. Before the creaking of the sign would begin again. Before Billy Grady came to him in his dreams.

On his upturned trunk, Timms dropped the ash from his pipe into his hand and blew it away as dust. Evangeline had followed him into the woods and trod uneasily from side to side. "I'm here girl, easy now." He stood and pressed his head against her snout. She nuzzled him and nibbled his collar. "Goddamn it, I know, I know…I promised I'd never leave." He walked the horse out of the woods and re-joined the trail.

"We'll camp here tonight."

Timms turned round before Corsair could see the wry smile on his face.

On the way to school

by Paul Clark

A trip that we take for granted

In weather hot and cool

Whether bus or shanks' pony

The journey to your school

Bike or a scooter

Or a rolling hoop

Consider the crocodile

Or another type of group

A schoolboy in Africa

Has to navigate the signs

Along with vicious wildlife

He has to spot the mines

So let your son or daughter

Know how lucky they are

Beware of the dangers

They are sure to go far

Overseas Experience

by Martyn Kempson

She was all noise and throbbing speed

a kiwi jet boat on a London pond.

Up for anything and no brakes,

Her body a theme park not a temple.

A Pension in Paris, a palazzo in Padua

a flat in Florence, a chalet in Gstaad

I took the ride with scary thrills.

Back on her home river.

In the land of the long white cloud

She proved tame as a punt on the Cam.

Travels

by Paul Clark

It's not just miles I travel
I seem to swim through time
I get caught in currents
In pools I gather slime.

The rocks mid-stream
I struggle to avoid
Rolling over rapids
So bruised and annoyed

I hope to reach the ocean
Rest on a sandy shores
With a book or two
A voyage to the Azores

When I read and write
I travel far beyond
But then return at last
To my sacred pond.

Westwood Ho!

by Martyn Kempson

Bleary vision through grimey glass.

On sodden runway flat fields

hay like Swiss rolls bound in plastic

sits on deserted pastures.

A station. Two. Then a manicured sward

with tractors vacuuming golf balls

to be endlessly recycled

A glimpse of swans on rush choked waters

as tangled maned horses grazing

in stubborn fields corralled by brambling hedges.

Over the bridge, redshank and egrets on mudflats below

and on through sullen grey Newport,

hard by blackened warehouses

and buddleia on broken paving

and so to terminus.

Unexpected

F.O.M.O.

by Bob Bootman

Think I'm feeling F.O.M.O.

All my friends are going out

Stuck inside, self-isolation

Covid rules, I mustn't flout

Sometime since I let my hair down

Although I haven't got much hair

Looking forward to a night out

And I don't think that it's fair

That my son went to a festival

And now is feeling crap

Tested positive for the virus

I was pinged by the covid app

Contact could be contagious

10 more days of staying in

You would think that I'd be used to it

But now it's wearing thin

Wish I could sit around a table

Down a pint and have a meal

It's been so long since I did it

Not too sure how I would feel

Surrounded by Cov-idiots

Anti-vaxxers fueling fear

Caution could be the best course for me

Better off remaining here

In my house I know that I am safe

One day, confident to roam

F.O.M.O. isn't the fear of missing out

It's the fear of missing 'ome

Bob Bootman (self-isolating 'til Wednesday)

Ice skating on Monday

by Bob Bootman

In the middle of not feeling well

I could hear the peel of a bell

My telephone singing

My ears, they were ringing

Was it someone with something to sell?

She said

"It's me, your best friend Trace,

Things are moving at a bit of a pace

With the guy I've been dating

We're going ice-skating

On Monday, d'you fancy a race?"

Was baffled and a little bemused

Had made me completely confused

I felt rather queer

No Tracey lived here?

The girl became quite amused

"This happens, in your defence

Your ears compact with wax that's dense

Here's what I'm fearing

You're losing your hearing

I'll speak up and it'll make sense.."

She repeated

"IT'S PHOEBE, FROM TEST AND TRACE

THOUGHT WE'D RING YOU, JUST IN CASE

WE KNOW IT'S FRUSTRATING

THAT YOU'RE ISOLATING

'TIL MONDAY

YOU MUST STAY IN YOUR PLACE"

F***ing Covid.....

Mother Goose

By Nicola Warner

Lizzie had her daughter Penny at a young age, although she never regretted having her daughter and could never imagine her life without her, she would often search the internet for a short cut into parenting. Lizzie hated reading to Penny at night, it brought more stress than enjoyment. Lizzie would read, Penny would ask questions or add her own spin to the story, which distracted Lizzie from reading, and she would often end up reading the same sentence more than once. It was irritating. On her nightly routine of online shopping, she found this cute, fluffy storyteller that resembled the loveable Mother Goose. She thought it was adorable. Her mother on the other hand didn't share the same views, she thought it was creepy, and made her feelings clear about buying unnecessary items that Penny just didn't want or need.

Lizzie still lived at home with her mother, who would help as often as she could, but sometimes felt like the live-in babysitter, which she probably was, as she would never say no. She loved the company.

The package arrived the next day right in the middle of its estimated time slot. Lizzie could hardly contain herself and shoed Penny off when she started asking too many questions.

"It's a surprise for bedtime!" Lizzie explained.

Penny gasped and jumped on the spot, "ok, I will go to my room and play!" Penny scurried off; with her hands clenched by her mouth I really hope mummy got me that night light I wanted! She thought to herself as she bounced into her bedroom to clear a space by her bed.

Bedtime was 7.30pm, and Penny hopped happily onto her bed after getting into her pyjamas and waited eagerly for her mum to bring in the surprise.

"Ok, close your eyes!" her mum teased as she tiptoed towards her bedroom door, "are they closed?"

"Yes, they are closed!" Penny squeaked.

Her mother stepped into the room quickly and placed the surprise beside her bed, "Ok, treacle, you can open your eyes!"

Penny let out a squeal and opened her eyes. Her face dropped, "Oh," she said quietly. That was not what she wanted, it had tatty fur, no feathers, its eyes were big and frosty, with harsh eyelashes, its beak was partially closed revealing the pink tongue inside, and it was wearing a dusky blue and pink bonnet with a matching large bow round its neck. Penny couldn't help but stare into its eyes … the large frosty blue eyes stared straight back at her, sending a shiver down her back.

"It's a storyteller, darling! Don't you love it!" She

lifted its wing, "look, you put your story disk in here …
and press play."

Lizzie said her goodnights and left the room.

A piercing scream alerted Lizzie and her mother to
Penny's room that night.

It was empty.

Silent.

Mother Goose perched on Penny's bed, "Its eyes
flickered as the mechanisms churned inside, "Would you
like to hear a story?"

The Trial

by Paul Clark

It was a volleyball evening like any other; but different. Very different. I'd been training with a national league team very Tuesday for the past three months. The area of Luton was called Hightown which was the exact opposite description of the sports hall!

Tonight was my debut with the local league division team to play against the main rivals in the league based in Bedford.

Both teams entered the hall and the din rose with screams and drum rhythms. The match, let alone the warm up hadn't started. Our captain set up our normal drills and welcomed me in the new team set up.

The match started. IT was close.

We won three sets to two and I had played a major role in the battle. In the days following an article appeared in the local rag as Bedford GNG had been unbeatable in the five seasons since the team entered the competition.

It had been a trial. The coach was looking for his national league squad; by invitation only for the elite Thursday evening training. It looked like I was in!!

And this is what still comes up in discussions thirty years later. In fact I was given a card for my 50th birthday at Luton Hoo with a laminated match report and article by the captain.

After the match the changing rooms were awash with cheers and whoops of joy. I was expecting the coach to come and tell me whether I had the green light to join the squad. I asked the captain; he didn't know. For the next five minutes , felt longer, the questions from the whole squad of 12 was "Are you in ?" I said I didn't know.

In the end I thought I'd ask him myself . There was no gushing but John , the coach in his low Irish brogue said "you are in Paul" and the merest hint of a wink!

Voices

Asking for it

by Bob Bootman

Why her?
It was her own fault.
There is no way
She wasn't asking for it.

It's her choice
The way she dresses
You would think
She wanted to be sexually abused

You can't say
She didn't enjoy the experience
All those drugs in her drink
How can you put
The blame on anyone else
You can't pass
Judgement....
She
Has
Cried rape before

(Now read bottom to top)

Conversations

by Nicola Warner

"You keep attempting that and I am going to pass out from laughing!"

"Good, at least I will have some peace!"

"Charming, is that the attitude I get for trying to help! It's a waste of time, you know all that, no one will be interested."

"You're not helping anyone. Don't listen, you have worked hard for this."

"It's pretty relentless, hard not to take notice."

"Block it out!"

"Easier said than done!"

"HA! Like she could get rid of me! I'll always be here! The voice of reason!"

"Voice of reason, my arse, all your doing is putting her down!"

"I'm getting to you too, aren't I?"

"You're annoying me, if that's what you mean."

"It won't be long!"

"What?"

"Watch!"

"Urgh!! I can't do this!"

"Finally, she has come to her senses!"

"Pay no attention, you can do this!"

"I can't believe I have wasted all this time!"

"Its only wasted if you give up, keep going!"

"Jeez what great advice, waste even more time."

"Shut up!"

"I'm so tired!"

"Then sleep, it will still be there in the morning."

"… And so will I!"

Miserable Mike

by Bob Bootman

Local groups on Facebook like

To include a moaning, miserable Mike

Spots everything like a 'Neighbourhood Ninja'

He's a weak and woeful, whining, whinger

"There's someone's bin outside my door

Who's playing music at half past four?

Why do people let their babies cry?

Is that smoke from a bonfire, I can spy?

Too many cars are pavement parking

Fed up with a dog's continuous barking

A Volkswagen Golf keeps driving too fast

Can we go back to living in the past?"

Would prefer to return to '54

He could leave unlocked his own front door

With his toilet placed inside his shed

Neighbours and family were all in-bred

No 'foreigners' living in the town

He feels they've brought the area down

Makes a statement of patriotic pride

With his Union Jack flying high outside

With his grumbling, groaning, growling views

Won't make any friends with his local news

He'll post on Facebook while he can

You would think he'd be a lonely man

But that isn't the case, what I find amazing

Many people agree with the points he's raising

There's lots of locals that seem to 'like'

The posts of moaning, miserable Mike

Miserable Mike part 2 – Wake Up call

Mike's post showed he was feeling blue

"Someone's given me the Wuhan flu

Just had a positive lateral flow

How I caught it, I really don't know?

Might have been the Asian girl next door

Or the Indian bloke at sixty-four

Could've been that do-gooder Sarah

Who drops off me shopping and got me a carer"

Some people commenting felt sorry for Mike

Shocked emojis and several likes

Another took a slightly different tack

He'd seen Mike out and didn't hold back

"I've seen you several times at the social club

And with your mates at the local pub

Complaining that the corner shop did ask

If you went inside, please wear a mask"

Mike didn't reply, like he'd disappeared

The truth was what he really feared

An ambulance called a little later

Now fighting for his life on a ventilator

Just about pulled through, it could've been worse

But for Doctor Gupta and Shazia, a nurse

They applied their skills and the medication

With experience, care and dedication

As Mike recovered, he recognised his saviours

One lived on his street, the other, his neighbour

He arrived back home after another week

Opened up his computer, it was time to speak

"That fucking covid nearly had me floored

I was the only white person on the ward

Bloody immigrants are ruining this town"

And his Facebook page was taken down

Taking a Break

by Martyn Kempson

The following poem was inspired by a conversation overheard in David's coffee shop, Letchworth.

Spring 2021

"I can't say I'm impressed" said the stout woman with the blue face mask worn half hanging off her ear.

"You'd think they could sort it better as we've been waiting since half past ten"

"It was the same yesterday" said the woman in the green coat "perhaps we should try the new one with the chairs outside. They've got parasols"

The half- masked woman moaned "They don't let you bring dogs inside though so it's no good for me and Brutus. Not with my condition. I can't leave him at home else he will chew the carpets"

"Yes, I forgot "said blue mask" you don't like sitting outside since you had that thing up at the Lister"

"Here's our drinks now" said the Green Coat" They drank slowly and silently.

"Same time tomorrow then?

They laughed.

Taking a Break

Fifty years ago, in school

we huddled in a corner

sharing Wagon Wheels

and our education.

Now more solid figures

we sip lattes and

share our company.

The Dinner Party

by Tina Cooper

'Good evening, your grace. Let me take your cloak. This way, the others are already seated. Keen to try the game pie I promised them I think.'

'Ha! Indeed. Did my dear friend make it?'

'I'm afraid not. Too cold to travel apparently. Can't think why they call him the man for all seasons.'

'Good evening everyone. Please sit, no need for formalities this evening.'

'Good evening, your grace.'

'Good evening, your grace. How was your journey?'

'Not bad. A little bumpy but that's the way of a carriage I suppose. The roads bear little forgiveness at this time of year. Had it not been for the rain I should have ridden here myself.'

'Catherine not with you?'

'No. This is court business. I am no longer including Catherine in matters of the court as she is not of sound judgment. Catherine is unwell. Mary is with her.'

'Mary? Is that Anne's sister? Anne is a bonny wee thing.'

'Anne is the reason I called this meeting.'

'Oh. Do tell. Getting tired of Mary are we?'

'Haha, you sure Mary does not tire of him?'

'Stop it you fools! I'll not have you speak of Anne in this way. This is a matter of great importance, to you, to me and to the country. I need your help with…'

'My apologies, your grace. That is the door. Cannot think who would be calling, uninvited, at this hour.'

'Oh, Good evening sir. We didn't think you would make it.'

'Why ever not? I am his most humble friend and advisor. I should be here above all others.'

'Of course sir. Forgive me. Through here.'

'Hurrah. Thank heavens you are here, the voice of reason. Sit. Sit. I brought ale. Now, to the matter of which I have you all gathered here. I wish to marry Anne. No. I will marry Anne. However, this will not be an easy endeavor as the Pope refuses to dissolve my marriage to Catherine. Some nonsense about Charles being her nephew. I need your help to find a way around this, legal or otherwise, and soon. I will not wait a moment longer than is necessary. Any objections? Thomas, as my dearest and most trusted friend, can you, nay, will you help me rid myself of the dour

Catherine in favour of my truest love, Anne?'

'Of course, your grace. As your friend and ally in all things I will do everything in my power to get you that which your heart most desires. I believe that Anne will make a good and fair queen. The people will love her as they do you. All in favour of Henry becoming Supreme Head on earth of the Church of England say aye.'

'Aye, your grace.'

'Aye.'

War Poetry

Blood on their hands

by Bob Bootman

When the bombs start dropping
Machine guns popping
Who decides who is to die?
Not you
Or I
Generals and politicians
In privileged positions
Wielding their power
From their ivory tower
Send us to foreign lands
With blood on their hands
We are
Pawns
In their game of chess
This preposterous mess
Wading in mud
Mixed with guts and blood
Sharing trenches with rats
As guns rat-a-tat-tat
Losing the passion
Hungry with meagre rations

"Your king and country need you"
And this is how they feed you?

Why?
What is it for?

This endless
War

I cry at the sight
Of us losing the fight
As friends around me
Die each night
We are
Lambs to the slaughter
My best mate Jack
Leaves a wife
And a daughter

I don't understand
Is it really
'Sweet and fitting to die for the homeland?'

How will it end?
When will it stop?
A cry goes up
To go over the top
Climb the ladder again
Then comes the pain
Feel my breathing cease
The sweet release
And finally
I
Can
Rest in Peace

Mines and Memories

by Paul Clark

Both just below the surface

Both are on the rise

The first we spot with eyes

Second never dies

Some mines are found

On a beach in a wood

Or by a drone

Many more are sown

Cropping all year round

A most pernicious weed

It chokes out life

Dark memories are rife

November the 11th

From 1917

Memories and mines

Still a danger in modern times

To those we lost, we thank you

by Tina Cooper

Thankfully I wasn't there

Nor were any that I love

A horror I cannot imagine

A fear I know not of

Many brothers, sisters, fathers, sons

Died not knowing that they'd won

They'd kept us safe from harm

We were safe because they'd gone

Grateful is not enough

A "thank you" can barely touch

The sacrifice they made for us

Their families gave too much

Lives lost to keep our freedoms

Freedoms we ignorantly cherish

I hope that future generations learn

For what those lives did perish

Fortunate are our children

Who can choose which battles to fight

Be it climate change or racism

I hope they try to do what's right

We get our chance to make the world

A better place to be

Because of those that came before

Honour them, live happily/gratefully/hopefully

William's Poem – The offspring of Tina Cooper

People fighting for their lives, slowly heading for demise

Open battlefields full of the dead, every puddle running red

Paralyzed bodies repeatedly shot, years beyond their corpses will rot

Plumes of smoke fill the air, neither side has any care

Immobilized bodies squirming in pain, rolling in mud, going insane

Entering through the pearly gates, people starting to meet their fates

Sad days and years ahead, thinking of those who are now dead

You Can Tell the Men
by Martyn Kempson

You can tell the men
who've been there
by the way they don't tell
of dropping in Arnhem
Into a burning hell.
Some walked away
behind the grinding tanks
just looking to survive
and not expecting thanks.
And he's on the road again
as he's gathered to advance
for another ten miles in
his bit of muddy France.
The Sergeants bully and cajole
while he's hiding by the road side
and cowering in a hole.
And he won't tell his children
that he's killed with gun and knife
and screamed, sobbed and cried
as his friends and foes died.
And in his mind he closed the door
and shut it out for evermore.

Xmas

Choc Early for Christmas

by Paul Clark

To get into the party mood

I have been out to shop for food

Twix I have duly selected

Away from Mince Pies, deflected

It's a limited edition

It could be a new tradition

It's Winter Spice

A literary naval splice

I get no commission

In future, no omission

A treat of confection wares

Yes, I'd like to buy some shares!

Only one Winter Spice Twix was eaten during this composition!

Santa Claus is Coming to Town

by Nicola Warner

Liz loved this time of year. The sharp chill in the air, the lights that invaded every street in town illuminated the houses in Christmas spirit, and not forgetting the mulled wine, or any wine for that matter, Christmas was the best excuse to celebrate, "drink and be merry!"

This year was going to be a tiny bit different. Tiny being the small bundle named Caleb gurgling away to himself in his bouncy chair by the sofa. Liz never really used to appreciate the open plan of the living room and kitchen until now. She liked that she could move him far away enough from the oven and anything sharp, but she could still keep and eye on him, she liked to think that he liked that he could still see her too. She still couldn't get her head around the fact that she was now a mother, everything was still so new to her, but she was pretty sure being that kind of merry this year wouldn't go down too well. This year's motto will have to be "be merry, but don't drink!" Still, she had the Christmas markets to look forward to, and was excited to take a teething 12-week-old to see Father Christmas today. Maybe he was a little young for it, but her sister, Lesley, was taking her two girls, Tilly and Lara, and she thought she would tag along. She didn't get to see her sister often. Two years ago she moved to London with her boyfriend, Andrew, and father to her youngest. She was looking forward to seeing her sister, they were close before she moved away, and she hadn't left the house much since her fiancé had returned to work. It was lonely - it would be good to get out for the day.

***

"I've just realised why I don't go out anywhere, feel how heavy his changing bag is!" she wobbled over to her sister.

"Ha! Be thankful you're breastfeeding, imagine having to cram in clean bottles and those mini cartons of formula!"

"Do people breastfeed in public?" she asked hastily, "I'm not sure what the procedure is."

"When he's hungry just whack 'em out love, if anyone has a problem, I'll sort them out." She stood laughing as she started to imitate a form of masculinity.

"Well, maybe we can find somewhere discreet then, I wouldn't want to ruin our day out by causing offence to the wives of the men with wandering eyes."

Her sister laughed, "how do you think I found baby daddy number 2?" she winked, "come on we best make a move, you don't want to be attempting to balance bags, baby and boobs while in that queue, it could get ugly!"

***

Lesley's children squealed as they pulled into the carpark, while Caleb was sound asleep in his car seat, "Mummy look, look! There are elves! ... tall elves, I thought they were small? Mummy, is this really where Father Christmas lives? Are we at the north pole?" Tilly squeaked.

Lesley rolled her eyes, "No, they aren't elves - they are ... 'helpers'. The elves are at the factory making and wrapping presents ready for the big day! And no, this isn't the north pole, this is Father Christmas' ... er ..."

"Holiday house!" Liz interrupted triumphantly.

Lesley looked at her gratefully, "Yes! That's right! Holiday house! This is his holiday house, well remembered Aunty Liz!"

"Well, I'm still learning!"

"What do you mean learning?" Lara questioned, "do you not believe in Father Christmas? You should you know!"

"Oh no, of course I believe in Father Christmas!" she said shifting her eyes over to her sister, "speaking of which, should we go and make sure we are all on the right side of this list he keeps checking?"

***

"Well, that was an experience, he slept all the way round the winter wonderland, then screamed like a psychopath having his photo taken!"

"To be honest, I don't blame him, who hires a guy that smells like stale spirit?" Lesley screwed up her face and whispered, "You could smell him a mile off!"

"Hmm ... should I sanitize him?" she asked wiping Caleb's little hands with a wet wipe.

"Don't worry he will be fine! Should we grab a coffee and a cake from the café before we go?"

"Great idea, he's due a feed." She said as they walked towards the café.

"Can always ask Santa to give him another cuddle, fumes would knock him out for a while!" Lesley joked.

"I think that borders on child abuse!"

"At least you could drink your coffee hot! I'm thinking of taking mine back round! ... Hi! Can I have two lattes and two hot chocolates please ... aaaand ... four chocolate muffins, thank you!"

"Here, take my card," Liz offered while she was fumbling through her bag.

"Don't be silly, I'll get these. You go and find us a table, looks like someone is getting restless!" Lesley pointed at her nephew who had now started throwing his arms about and making weird snorting noises.

Liz ushered her nieces over to a quiet table tucked away in the corner, as the little terror started to demonstrate his lack of patience. She settled on the bench and popped the button on her shirt and guided the baby towards his feed, he latched on forcefully, which she wasn't expecting him to do. As he was feeding she shifted and looked around the room awkwardly searching for someone's disapproving eye. Thankfully no one seemed to take much notice.

"Here we go!" Lesley set a tray of steamy drinks and chocolate muffins on the table, "I had them put yours in a takeaway cup, just in case."

"Great, thank you." Liz smiled as she picked at a chocolate muffin.

"Girls, I got you hot chocolates. Maybe let them ?"

"OW!" Tilly cried.

"... cool down," Lesley continued, shaking her head, "Eat your cake first Tilly."

"So... what have you asked Father Christmas to bring you this year?" Liz smiled.

"Hopefully baby daddy number 3!"

"You are kidding? What happened with Andrew?"

"Oh we broke up a while ago. Fancied his secretary, so I told him to go for it, wished him all the best in a very elegant styled bitch fit, threw a plate to guide him out and off he popped. He wasn't interested in a life with me and the girls."

"Oh, wow, I'm sorry, I didn't know!"

"Why would you?"

"Mummy is it cool now?" Tilly moaned.

"I don't know, try it."

"OW! It's still hot!"

Lesley rolled her eyes, "Try blowing it a bit before you take a sip, finish your cake."

"But it's making me thirsty!"

Lesley rolled her eyes again, "just eat the cake!"

Lesley turned her attention back to her sister, "I didn't really tell anyone, wasn't a big deal... I'm actually seeing someone new."

"You should have told me. We're sisters."

"He had made his choice." She smiled.

"So, what's the new guy like? Is he coming to mum's for Christmas?"

Well, he's ... mysterious. I'm not even sure it will go anywhere... He's um ... kind of ... engaged to someone else."

Liz's mouth fell open, "what? You are joking?

What the hell are you playing at?"

"Oh relax, it's just a bit of fun. Anyway, enough about me. How is your love life? Have you set a date yet? And am I actually going to meet this guy before the wedding?" her sister laughed.

"Of course you will! You shouldn't live so far away. Things are ... ok ... I guess."

"Just ok? Something going on?"

"Mummy, can you blow this so it's cool?"

"Don't be such a wimp, its not even hot now!" Lara teased.

"Is too!"

"Is not!"

"Girls!" Lesley barked as she took the mug from Tilly who was claiming it was still too hot to drink, and started to blow into it, "Sorry, Liz, you were saying?"

"He just works all the time at the moment. It seems like he is taking on every business trip he is offered," she sighed, "he doesn't even seem interested in Caleb. He's so distant."

"Bin him." Lesley ordered, "Get rid, and come and live with me."

"And be witness to your family affairs," she

laughed, "I think I will stay put."

"Mummy, is it cool now?"

"It should be fine now," she passed the mug back to her daughter, "When she has finished that we will make a move, yes? Is he still feeding?"

Liz looked down, "Nope, he is out for the count. Might have just enough time to down my luke warm latte .... yummy."

"I could always ask them to chuck some ice in there?" Lesley suggested.

"Oh god no, far too cold for that."

***

The landline echoed around the house bang on 7.00pm, as it did every night.

"Hello?"

"Hi Babe."

The sound of his voice made her smile, "When are you coming home?"

"Couple of days maybe, could even be another week, everything ok? Little man ok?"

"Oh right. I was hoping you would be home to help get the decorations out of the loft, I wanted to get the place decorated ... otherwise there won't be much point. It's Caleb's first Christmas."

"Well it's not like he'll notice, look I'll help when I get back, ok?"

"Yeah, except you don't know when that will be."

"Babe. Don't start."

"Well, it's true!"

"It's just a couple of days, ok? I'll call you tomorrow."

"Ok... I'll speak to you tomorrow... I lov-"

She sat quietly on the side of the bed, trying her best to hold back tears that were falling fast, she took in a deep breath, wiped her eyes and returned the phone to its charger. Her mobile pinged next to her ...

[Hey, mum said she would watch the kids for a couple of hours tomorrow. Bring Caleb round, we'll do something]

[How are you at climbing into lofts?]

[That's how you want to spend your childfree time? Can't Ethan do that?]

[He's not coming home for a few more days. Not sure when. So he says ;( ]

[Pack Caleb's bag. Mum's going to pick him up at noon, she's offered a trip to the park haha! I'll jump in with her and come to yours]

[Please don't say anything to Mum]

[As if. She's still asking if Andrew is coming for Christmas dinner Haha! I'm avoiding the subject. See you tomorrow]

***

"Lying to the Mrs ... They don't like that you know!"

Ethan turned to his colleague, "Dan, the day I come to you for relationship advice, hell will have frozen over."

"I'm just saying mate, I've screwed a lot of girls around to know how they think, I even have some of it in writing!" He said as he waved his phone at him, "and 9 times out of 10 they are bang on the money! Imagine the first conclusion she is going to come to with all these hours you're putting in, I heard the boss man tell you it wasn't necessary for you to take on the extra work. So what's that about?"

"Not really got much to do with you, has it?"

"Just offering some friendly advice!" He held his hands in the air in defence, "just think about what it is you want, you are supposed to be marrying this girl. You have a kid."

"Exactly what is it you are trying to accuse me of?"

"Exactly what she will be thinking, mate! Think about it, yeah!"

Ethan frowned at him.

"Pub in half an hour? It's Blake's round ... again," Dan laughed.

Ethan nodded, "sure."

***

"There's spare clothes in here, his soother, a few toys, and I've expressed some milk, should be good for a few hours yet. Will you be ok? I'll just go and get his pushchair. Do you need me to show you how to unfold it?"

"Eliza! I have done this before! We'll be fine!" her mother assured, "I'll pop him in his car seat, you bring the pushchair outside, I'm sure I can figure it out!"

Liz and Lesley waved as their mum drove off. "So where's this loft then?" Lesley asked.

"It's literally at the top of the stairs." Liz closed the front door and showed Lesley the loft hatch.

"You weren't kidding! It is literally at the top of the stairs, how the hell are we going to get into that without breaking our necks?" Lesley questioned as she studied the area.

"Ladder?" Liz suggested.

"Where the hell would you position it?"

"Well, you only need it to get to that hook there to open it, there is a ladder attached up there on the flappy thing." She gestured.

"Flappy thing?" Lesley chuckled. "Isn't there usually a pull cord if there is a ladder?"

"Yes. There was. Ethan snapped it."

"Brilliant."

Liz left Lesley puzzled at the top of the stairs and went to retrieve the ladder from the cupboard in the kitchen.

"Um ... is that ladder big enough?" Lesley asked hesitantly.

"It was the last time Ethan went up there. We only need it to reach the hatch." Liz positioned the ladder against the wall. "Right, up you go, I'll keep hold of the end."

"Me?! It's your bloody loft!"

"Oh go on, please!"

"Fine! But if I die, you will be the first person I'm coming back to haunt!"

Liz laughed, "you're not going to bloody die." She smirked as she quickly stamped her hands on the foot of the ladder.

Lesley Shrieked, "Oh my god! Don't do that you cow!"

Liz laughed, "I'm sorry, but you would have done the same to me."

"If I fall, I'm aiming for you!"

"Have you unhooked the latch yet?" Liz asked, trying to hold back the giggles.

"No, I haven't. If you weren't trying to rattle me to my death I'd have done it by now."

"Oh calm down, drama queen! I won't shake it again, promise!"

"There, done it. Now do I just pull? Is this ladder attached to the door going to roll out on me?"

"No, there is a latch you pull to release the ladder, but don't do that while you are up there."

"Can we reach the latch without the ladder I'm balancing on?"

"Um..." Liz shrugged.

"Oh for god's sake, I'm just going to pull the latch and guide the ladder down, as I come down this one."

"Won't this ladder get in the way?"

"I guess we will find out!" Lesley grinned as she unlatched the safety on the loft ladder and slowly guided it down with her.

"Lesley, wait a minute, that's going to -"

CLUNK!

"Oh bloody hell!"

"- get stuck." Liz covered her face, "now what?"

"If I lift the loft ladder back up you pull out the other ladder and just slide it over."

"Oh 'just slide it over' you make it sound so easy... what if it slips and takes me down the stairs with it?"

"Well after I've finished wetting myself, I will ring you an ambulance, ok?"

Liz stared at her unimpressed.

"Well, if it starts to slide down, just jump out of the way," Lesley suggested with a grin.

"Do I look like Tom Cruise to you?"

"Stop moaning. Are you ready?"

"As ready as I will ever be!"

"Ok, I'll lift, you pull, ready? Go!"

Liz burst into an uncontrollable fit of giggles, and creased to her knees at the bottom of the ladder, wheezing a word to herself. Pivot!

"What is wrong with you?" Lesley frowned at her.

"PIVOT!" she spat louder.

Lesley stared at the giggling ball curled up on the stairs struggling to catch its breath.

"Pivot!" Liz howled, "get it?"

Lesley tried to keep a straight face, then broke at her sisters flushed face. Her eyes were streaming, "only you!" she laughed, "you know this isn't a sofa don't you?"

"Yes I know, sorry, I just had an image in my head, and it just reminded me of..." Liz breathed trying to control herself. She wiped her eyes quickly, "OK, Wooo! I'm ready. Let's go!"

The two of them got in position, Lesley lifted the loft ladder up while Liz shuffled the other ladder along in loud clatters. Lesley guided the loft ladder to a stable position with ease, "see, it was easy!" she hailed.

"I really hope there's a light up there," Liz stated nervously

"Well you should know, it is your house!"

"I've never been up there, and Ethan has only been up there once to shove bits and bobs up there when we moved in."

"So you have no idea where anything is?"

"Nope!"

"Maybe I should text mum to see if she can keep the kids longer?"

"Ethan will have put the Christmas stuff in one pile, it would aggravate his brain if he didn't. It should be easy to find. You go first!"

"God, you are a wimp! Come on!"

Liz hesitantly, followed Lesley up the ladder into the loft, "Have you found a light switch?"

Lesley tapped her hand around the side of the wall, "Yes!" she cheered as she flicked the switch, "Come on wimp you have no excuse now." Lesley called over the hole in the floor.

Liz climbed up slowly, and brushed off cobwebs she thought were clinging to her arms, "Urgh, I hate cobwebs." She shivered.

"How lucky are you that this has all been boarded! I had images of us beam balancing!"

"And legs dangling from ceilings!"

"Oh that's a shame, we could have had the firemen out to rescue us!"

"Always on the prowl for baby daddy number 3!" Liz taunted.

Lesley scowled at her, "Hey, look at this lovely pile of boxes here marked 'Christmas' - are you taking all of them down?"

"Might as well ... how do we get them down ... there?"

"We carry them down?" Lesley sniggered, "have you really never done this before?"

"Yes ... but I normally stand at the bottom of the ladder and wait for Ethan to bring it all down." She smiled innocently.

"Come on Princess, let's get these downstairs!"

***

Liz made her way over to the fridge, and retrieved a cold bottle of Zinfandel, "I think I owe you a drink! Want a glass? As long as you don't feel weird about drinking by yourself?"

"You're not having a glass? Really?"

"No, I best not, I really hate expressing milk, so I

will drink the fake stuff, and even that has a placebo effect!"

"Oh, God. Go on then, pour me one!" she dramatized.

"It was nice of mum to say she would take the girls for the night, they could have stayed too."

"And miss a childfree night away?"

"Well, it's not completely child free, Caleb's here," Liz laughed.

"Yeah, but he's not going to cause any trouble is he, didn't you say he was starting to sleep through?"

"Well, not completely, he does let me have a decent sleep though, but he will wake up about midnight for a feed."

"That's plenty of time to for us to catch up!" she beamed as she accepted the large glass of rosé, "with ice! You remembered! Thank you very much!"

"You are the only person I know that gets excited over ice in their drink."

"You should see the looks I get in the local when I ask for ice in my wine, itis refreshing not being stared at like I have two heads."

"I reserve judgment!" Liz chuckled.

Lesley stared at the boxes from the loft they had struggled to carry down the ladder, "I hope nothing is broken in that one you dropped!"

"It wasn't my fault, I told you I wasn't ready for another, and you dropped it straight down the ladder. Could have knocked me out!"

"... But it didn't," Lesley smirked.

"Well, as grateful as I am for your bad aim, you're still going to help me go through these boxes."

Lesley looked back at the boxes and pulled an agonised expression, "I'm going to need more wine!"

They began to open the boxes one by one, starting with the box that Lesley shot down the ladder. Liz smiled at the memories that were tucked away in them and pulled out a gold macaroni star drowned in glitter that her nieces had made together the year she got her first flat. She was a little anxious about living alone for the first time, so they had told her it would protect her, "oh look. Do you remember when they made me this? They were so small!"

"Oh my god, you kept that rubbish! Ours went in the bin straight after new year!"

"Lesley!" Liz gasped.

"What?" she laughed, "it was half eaten, and the glitter was falling off! Clearly they took more care while making yours!"

"I loved it. It was so sweet of them." Liz smiled.

"Where on earth did you get this?" Lesley shrieked as she glared into a black bin bag, "it's creepy!"

"What is it?"

Lesley turned to Liz, a little horrified, and showed her an old Santa doll. It had a plump plastic face with puffy cheeks and a bulbous nose that was a fading dull pink. The paint that had once highlighted Santa's trademark white beard had rubbed down bare in areas. Its coat was tatty and the white trimming was discoloured. The only part that retained colour was its bright blue static eyes. Liz stared at it puzzled.

"It's staring into my soul! If this is what 'sees me while I'm sleeping' I'm getting a taxi home!" Lesley tensed.

"I know it's a bit creepy, but that's a little dramatic." Liz laughed.

"Where did it come from?"

"I'm not sure, maybe it's something that belonged to someone in Ethan's family?" Liz shrugged.

"Well I suggest you bin it, or hide it, or something. That thing will give Caleb nightmares!" she protested as she shoved it back in the black bag, tying it closed with a double knot, "I'd like to see you get out of that creepy Santa!" she sneered, "here do something with it, get it out of here!"

Liz took the bag from Lesley with a chuckle, "And I thought I was the scaredy cat of the family!" she said as she placed the bag at a comfortable distance from her sister.

"Believe me, I have seen some creepy dolls in my time, but that one takes it home. There is just something off about it. I just can't put my finger on it!"

"Well I can't just chuck it, what if it's Ethan's great great grandmother's or something? I don't think that would go down too well with the In-laws to be."

"I'm sure they would get over it, just leave it waaay over there if it has to stay!"

"Would you like more wine?" Liz offered as a distraction.

"Yes! Please!"

Liz took Lesley's glass into the kitchen for her calming refill, while Lesley stared anxiously at the black bag.

"HERE YOU GO!"

"Lizzie!" Lesley gasped clutching her chest, "you cow! Scared me half to death!"

"Sorry, I couldn't resist!"

"I'm sure that bag moved."

"Oh don't be silly of course it didn't. Maybe I should put the kettle on?"

"I'm telling you, that bag moved!"

Liz stared at the bag with a sly smirk, "Oh... my... I think you're right!"

"What? No? You're not meant to agree!!"

"No... Oh my god ... did you see that?!"

"What? No? Lizzie!!" Lesley jumped further back into the sofa and huddled behind a cushion.

"It is! ... It's ... Oh my god!" Liz shuffled backwards onto the sofa with a look of horror drawn on her face, "Oh my god!" she shrieked repeatedly.

"Lizzie!" Lesley cried covering her face.

"Caleb's awake." Liz smirked as she glanced over to the baby monitor. He wasn't crying, she could see his eyes glistening through the screen.

"I hate you."

"I'll go bring him down for his feed," Liz said as she pushed herself to her feet.

"Good! I can use him as a human shield!"

"Will you be ok down here by yourself for a few minutes?"

Lesley poked out her tongue, "I'll be fine!" she tried to convince herself.

"Okay!" Liz giggled as she made her way towards the door.

Lesley shifted her eyes over to the bag again, "Wait!" she jumped up, "wait for me!" and bolted towards the door.

**

"Good morning!" Liz greeted her sister, whose hair looked like it had been backcombed by a rather angry bush.

Lesley squinted back at her through dark circles, "Coffee. Paracetamol." She mumbled.

"I did suggest putting the kettle on last night!" Liz reminded her smugly.

Lesley made a groan that Liz had only ever heard in episodes of The Walking Dead.

"Are we feeling a little of the drinkers remorse this morning?" Liz teased.

"Please can I have some coffee!" Lesley whined while she cradled her head. She glanced to the side and shot up very alert as if she had just been poked with something very sharp, or very hot, "what the hell is that doing here?"

Liz frowned, "what are you talking about?" she followed her sisters fear struck eyes, and froze. She couldn't quite muster a response.

"Seriously, Liz it wasn't funny last night and it's still not funny now!"

"I-I swear I didn't put it there. I purposely left it in the bag last night because it freaked you out so much, and I was going to wait until Ethan got home to find out where it came from!"

"Then how the hell did it get there?"

Santa sat. Staring straight into their eyes.

'You better watch out,

you better not cry,

you may want to run,

He'd like to see you try,

Santa Claus is coming to town.

He's making a list,

checking it twice,

He will find out if you deserve to be knifed,

Santa Clause is gonna hunt you down.

Now … Run!'

To tattoo or not to tattoo?

by Tina Cooper

That is the question.

Well, it is a question. It's probably not the question but it is a question nonetheless.

The answer, of course, is not.

We should not tattoo. They are painful, costly and ridiculous. They serve no purpose other than to have a giggle with the artist at the time of application and a damn good excuse to eat lots immediately afterwards*.

I have 14 tattoos and will have more. The thing is you can't have one, one is just the beginning, one is a practice. Can you take the pain? Will your tattoo artist give you what you want? Will it take well on your aging skin? Ha, nobody cares about that. Will you faint and make an arse of yourself?

The first, usually rather small, tattoo is just a trial run. You don't know this at the time but it is.

I had my first because my mum wanted one to remember her mum. An odd request as my mum doesn't like tattoos but grief is a funny friend who needs appeasing from time to time. I said I'd go with her and we both ended up with a simple heart. Commemorative tattoos are weirdly comforting, I can't explain it but they seem to help. It's all psychological of course but hey, whatever gets you through the day.

Mum went first and assured me it didn't hurt one bit.

The funny thing is that I believed her despite the fact that she once told me she was allergic to cats.

I'd wanted one as a child and was disappointed to hear of mum's allergy. I had to make do with Clarence, a shaggy black and white effort, from two doors up, who would let me pop him in the basket on the front of my bike and we would go on adventures together. Only to the end of the street but I was small, it felt like miles.

Fast forward roughly 20 years to mum stealing the neighbour's cat.

Tim had belonged to the neighbours daughter but when she left she didn't take him with her. I'm not sure how it happened but mum and the neighbours ended up sharing

Tim. It was mutual, you could tell by the Christmas cards.

To Glen, Bob, Tina and Tim (if he's there)

Merry Christmas from

Stan, Sheila and Tim (if he's here)

All was well until one fateful day Stan and Sheila moved to the next village.

Mum called me sobbing her heart out.

"They've taken Timmy. They swapped him for a box of chocolates! Bastards!"

Mum didn't really think that Stan and Sheila were bastards, honest, that was just the broken heart talking.

Tim hadn't been gone long when mum spotted Stan at his old house. Mum took the opportunity to run at him.

"Stan, hello, how's Tim? Oh and Sheila, is she well?" she rushed.

"Would you like us to bring Tim back? He's not really our cat so you can have him if you'd like?"

Mum did like.

That is how we ended up with a cat.

One evening we were doing the dishes, mum washing, and I was drying, when Tim said "ello." No, really. Tim could also say "ham" because he was a demon disguised as a fluff ball. Anyway… Tim wanted up so mum picked him up and snuggled into his neck.

"You're doing really well with Tim considering you're allergic to him," said I.

It was then that she gave me the look. At 27 years old the penny dropped. Mum wasn't allergic to cats at all.

So, you'll not be surprised to find out that mum was telling a fib, getting a tattoo does hurt.

Why have I got 14 of them then?

I have absolutely no idea.

I once stood, arm out, with my tattoo artist placing his artwork onto me when I asked him that very question.

"What sort of person goes on to have more tattoos when they know it hurts?" I asked as I was being prepped for my 6th.

"Well, it's mainly drug dealers and criminals," said the chap covered head to toe in tattoos.

"Ah, that explains it, I'm all of the above," I chuckled.

I still wonder which of the two he is. Perhaps I'll find out on the 29th December when I'm getting my next tattoo.

*if you're in the chair a while you can go a bit weak and watery. Top tip, take snacks.

'Twas the night before Christmas

by Bob Bootman

'Twas the night before Christmas, not bought her a present,

No pets in the pet shop, not even a pheasant;

The stockings were hung by the chimney with care,

My wife's one was empty, nothing was there;

The children were useless, no ideas did they give,

One suggested a whisk, the other a sieve;

Too late for Amazon, I have to disparage,

Had to go off to the local garage

Went out in the car with a bit of a clatter,

"What was that?" she cried, I said, "Doesn't matter!"

Away to the garage, I flew like a flash,

Tore open my pocket and took out my cash;

Started to search, not as easy as it sounds,

What can you get for twenty-two pounds?

When, what to my wandering eyes should appear,

But a shelf full of wine and a fridge full of beer;

With time moving on I had to be quick,

I thought for a moment, well, what could I nick?

More rapid than eagles, took a bottle of wine,

Stashed it into my trousers, well that'll be fine;

I then dashed and danced and stole a few more,

Bagged a good book and ran straight through the door;

Ran past a Porsche and jumped onto a wall,

Then up to the roof, on the tiles I did crawl;

As dry leaves flew on a cold north wind

Along the red ridge to a chimney I shinned;

On top of the house I drew my breath,

I then heard a sound which scared me to death;

With sirens wailing, I heard on the roof,

The prancing and pawing of each little hoof;

As I drew my head and was turning around,

On top of the chimney a policeman was crowned;

He was dress'd all in fur, from his head to his foot,

And onto his head, his helmet he put;

His sleigh was white with luminous stripes,

With sirens and lights of different types;

His eyes were bloodshot, bit like he'd been drinking,

His cheeks with red blusher, well what was he thinking?

His puckered-up mouth, just like a dog's bottom,

Was wearing no trousers, I think he forgot 'em;

Smoking a joint, was as high as a fairy,

A festival smell, just like Glastonbury;

He had a round face, and an over-large belly

Been drinking too much, like that bloke from the telly;

He slurred when he spoke and started to drool,

I sniggered and laughed, a little bit cruel;

A wink of his eye and a shake of his head,

He started to ramble, didn't know what he said;

He then started pointing whilst trying to speak,

The wine in my trousers had started to leak;

Tapped his nose with his finger and stared straight at me,

A little embarrassed by what he could see;

He said,"It's Christmas tomorrow, it mustn't be blighted,

I think that you've been naughty and got over-excited

I'll only give you a caution, because of your plight

Happy Christmas to all, and to all a good night…"

Epilogue….

I'd escaped, wasn't punished, though I'd mis-behaved,

Coz of drunken police Santa, my Christmas was saved,

I'll go home to the wife and tell her the truth,

But I slipped on the tiles and fell off the roof.

The End

Merry Christmas

Cut out this page and create a Christmas Card to
accompany this book if it is a gift.

Keeps on giving …

Yikes!

Karma's a bitch

by Nicola Warner

"Well, that was interesting. I've never seen him react like that before. A bit over the top if you ask me." Bob said to his assistant.

Bob was tall, handsome and very, very funny. He considered himself to be a tolerant man, but he had reached his limit for bullshit today. He watched as George walked down the corridor towards the exit, muttering curse words to himself, before turning and raising his middle finger as he left the building.

The day passed quickly, his employees tip-toed carefully around him, they didn't want to be next in the firing line. He always found the threat of unemployment a satisfactory technique to give everyone a productive kick up the backside. It was unfortunate, as George was a hard worker, but he just kept pushing for "a quiet word" and wouldn't take no for an answer.

He arrived home two hours later than what he had promised his wife, but this was nothing new and she had since given up with her complaints. As he approached his front door he noticed how quiet it was "that's odd, it doesn't look like she's home." He headed for the living room, maybe she had taken a nap that afternoon. She wasn't there. He looked around the room. Nothing seemed out of the ordinary. He noticed the curtain blowing gently and tutted, "bloody woman, fancy leaving the window open!" He pushed the curtain back. The window was broken. A brick lay on a bed of shattered glass. It had a note tied to it. As he went to untie the bow, he heard a sudden rustling from the kitchen. He was in darkness, it hadn't occurred to him to switch on a light. He would make a bolt for the front door and then ring his wife from outside. Congratulating himself on his cleverly diverse plan, he quietly made his way towards the door.

BANG!

Pain stretched through his leg. He tried to escape, scrambling for the doorway. He sensed the key before he felt it. As he looked behind him he saw the man lunge for his leg.

BANG!

The man fell to the ground with a piercing groan.

Bob looked up to see George placing a gun into a holster under his jacket, "w-what the hell are you doing here?" he demanded, nursing his leg, "and who the hell is that?!"

"He was apparently an exterminator from Pest Control. They don't normally carry guns. Very odd."

George calmly tapped the man with his foot. He winced and attempted to raise his head. So George looked hard at the thug, paused, took out his gun from its shoulder holster, thought again, and then shot him in the head.

"Y-you ... shot him ... in the h-head," Bob stuttered, "H-how ... W-why do you have a g-gun?"

George turned to a trembling Bob and smiled, "All part of the plan." He raised the gun again, this time pointing it at Bob.

"N-no p-please, I-I have family, my wife!"

George laughed, "your wife? Your wife and I have been having an affair. I tried to talk to you. You wouldn't give me the time. You chose the wrong guy to fire today, Bob,"

He smiled. "Now, not only do I have your wife, I'll have your home and your business!"

"Where is she?" Bob trembled.

"Oh don't you worry, she's perfectly safe. She's not been murdered... and now thanks to this guy, the house is now clear of vermin!" He winked.

"Goodbye, Bob." A quiet but stern voice said from the stairway.

Bob looked from George to his wife, "why?" he asked desperately.

BANG!

"Karma's a bitch!"

Using a Spratt to catch a Mackerel

by Bob Bootman

The cold wind whistled through George's long blond hair, as he stood outside the failing, soon to be closed-down, Off-Licence, in a dark corner of Harlow.

'Arfur Lager' had struggled ever since Tesco opened a superstore on the estate next door and the owner, Arthur Spigot, was getting desperate.

He had hired George to kill his wife, Sharon Spratt, so he could claim the insurance money, shut down the Off-Licence, and flee to Walton-On-The-Naze, with his long-time lover Beryl Mackerel.

Arthur couldn't afford a 'real' hit man, but he knew George was a cold-blooded killer.

George had worked for Rentokill for twenty-five years, and he was well-known, locally, as someone who would do anything for a bit of cash.

This was the first time George had been asked to kill a real person, a human being, and he was slightly nervous.

Rats and cockroaches were easy, but humans?

That would take a lot of poison and then there was the disposal of the body…

He strode into the shop, his leather coat swirled around his ankles. His staff, topped with a silver snake, clutched in his left hand.

He was no ordinary Rentokill employee, and he loved the theatre of his Lucius Malfoy-esque wardrobe. It felt menacing and it told his customers he meant business.

And today, for five hundred quid, he meant business.

The entry bell ding-a-linged as he pushed the door ajar and shouted "Hah!' as he marched towards the counter.

He wasn't expecting the scene that greeted him.

A young man, with a pair of his Mum's tights over his head was holding-up the store.

George recognised him immediately.

It was Brian Putrid from Winchester Close.

George had recently cleared a wasp's nest from his parent's house and Brian had tried to nick his tools while George was up in the loft.

Brian waved the flick-knife in George's face.

George just laughed and snarled "Put it away, before you hurt yourself, Brian"

Brian felt a bit stupid that he'd been rumbled, panicked, pointed towards the skirting board, and shouted "Rat!"

While George was momentarily distracted by another potential 'victim', Brian took the opportunity to grab a handful of fivers from the till and scarpered.

George's attention now turned to the woman cowering in the corner behind the tills.

Sharon Spratt.

George had always had a 'thing' for Sharon, ever since she'd shared her wotsits with him behind the bike shed at school. He'd also let her suck on his sherbet dab.

Why the hell did she end up with that weasel, Arthur Spigot?

He couldn't kill his childhood crush.

But there was £500 in cash at stake here and he'd already been paid £250 up front by Arthur.

George came up with a plan.

"Scream" he said

"Scream?"

"I'm supposed to kill you"

"Kill me?"

"Arthur's paid me to kill you, now scream and pretend I'm killing you"

"Why?"

"So I can carry you off into the sunset and we can start a new life together"

"How much is he paying you then?"

"£500"

"£500?? The cheap bastard. How are we going to run off into the sunset with £500? We'll only get as far as Chelmsford"

"I have more stashed away. Please Sharon, I've never forgotten your wotsits"

"And I can never forget your shiny red sherbet dab. Let's do it"

Sharon screamed and went limp. George threw her over his shoulder, carried her out of the shop, threw her into the back of the van, and drove off, heading east on the A414, sunset bound.

They were never seen again in Harlow and moved somewhere up the east coast.

Rumour has it, that a new pest control company in Suffolk, called 'The Verminator', is run by a man who looks a bit like the nasty bloke from Harry Potter.

They both lived happily ever after

Ps. Arthur never received the insurance money as he'd forgotten to pay the premium.

Beryl Mackerel spurned Arthur's proposal, as he had no money, and ran off with Gordon Ratchett, the local Tesco store manager.

Arthur consequently burned down the Tesco superstore and is now serving 20 years for arson, in HMP Hollesley Bay, not far from Walton-On-The-Naze.

The End

Zodiac

Wagon of Heaven, Part i:
Beast
by Lewis Green

Once, he was born beneath thicket and thorn. Once, he was born in the dark of a cave. Once, he was born under a hail of arrows. A crescent moon. Lastly, he was born of Hera's bitter jealousy and a father's love. *What troubles you, little one?* Ursa Minor blinks inconsolable in the night. *Look*, his mother says, *look*.

A million miles away, a bear stands proud. Ursa Minor watches him as he lifts his snout and sniffs first east and then west. He was there when the cub's mother was taken. He was with him when he blinked his way uncomprehendingly from the mouth of the cave. And he was there when he took the hunter's arm. He watched the little bear stand over his mother as she plumed her last bloody breath into the snow. He watched the bear taste the hunter's blood as it hung from his terrible maw in bright beads like berries. Muzzle and maw matted pink and now fully alone, more uncomprehending than ever. He saw everything that came before and will see everything that comes after.

The bear sits on his haunches and scans the sky above. His eyes rest on the blinking lights. *Stars* his mother called them. *That one*, she said, *is Ursa Minor, the wagon of heaven.* It blinks above – his distant cousin from the long-ago – a smattering of stars across a black tapestry draped over the edges of the world. For a shimmering instant, it seems the stars shine just a little brighter, a little stronger, before fading away again. The orphan bear sniffs again, free to roam wherever he chooses. Mountain, coast, river, cave. Everything the sky touches belongs to him now.

Everything beneath this veil of stars.

Wagon of Heaven, Part ii:
Man

Finland, 1862

They'd come from the east in the heart of a blizzard. Sixteen souls searching for the coast. They came across a small cabin, and their leader, an old sailor, stepped forward and called out, "Hello there."

No greeting came back.

"Hello…we are in need of a shelter for the night – until the blizzard passes."

Again, no voice came back.

He held his lantern aloft and approached the window. No face peered back from within. The old man only saw his own face reflected back at him, hollow and bearded in the lantern's glow.

"We'd better get inside…here hold this."

He passed over his lantern to the man next to him and tried the door handle. It didn't move so he slid his knife between the door and its frame and prised them apart. The door opened with a damp splitting sound and swung open on its hinges.

They stepped inside and peered into the gloom. No-one to be found. The cabin was made up of one large room, and off this room came two smaller ones – a scullery, and a store cupboard. The main room had a fireplace and they all set forth to find some kindling. They found a small amount in the store cupboard but apart from that it was bare. Perhaps it had stood empty for years. A fire was lit, and the sailors threw on it any clothing they could spare. Someone tore out the pages from a book in his satchel and threw those on the fire too. All sixteen souls sat against the skirting, listening to the breathing of the others. They were all too tired too speak. They just smoked and watched the fire in the grate. The old man stood and went to the window.

He rubbed a grimy circle in the glass with a patch of his sleeve and regarded the constellations above.

"You see that'n there?"

"We wouldn't be no good as sailors if we didn't know the polaris, old man."

At this they all chucked.

"Well", the old man continued, "take your eyes to the west of it and see that pan shape."

"Aye, we see it."

"They call that one Ursa Minor, the little bear."

A cough escaped from his throat before it rattled away back inside his chest somewhere.

"You want to know how he got up there?"

"We don't have much else to do 'til morning."

"Ok."

And this is the tale the old sailor told. He told of a great beauty and a great love affair. And with all great love affairs, somebody always pays a great price.

The goddess of the hunt was called Artemis, and Artemis was followed by a band of beautiful nymphs. The most beautiful of these was Callisto, who had sworn to remain chaste in order to please Artemis the goddess. The powerful god Zeus, upon seeing Callisto, fell madly in love with her. He disguised himself as Apollo, the brother of Artemis and seduced the mortal Callisto. They became lovers and she bore him a son, Arcas. Zeus' vengeful wife Hera found out about his infatuation with Callisto, and in order to protect her and keep her from Hera's reach, he turned her into a great bear. Callisto was forced to roam the forests and hide herself away from hunters…

Here the old man paused to re-fill his pipe. All around the room cigarettes flare and dim in the dark. He takes a ragged breath and continues his story.

Now, Callisto still had her human feelings and so couldn't make friendships with any of the other animals. It truly was a lonely existence for Callisto. Several years later, Arcas, now a young man, was hunting in the forest. He had heard tell of a great bear that howled the most pitiful sounds as it stalked the forests. He tracked the great bear over many days and over many miles, before he could get close enough to kill it. From his hiding place Arcas could see the great bear stop in its tracks and sniff at the air. He drew his bow and arrow and raised it to eye-level…

The old man paused again here to make sure they were still listening. A few soft snores had started in the corner of the room, but he could still see cigarettes and pipes blazing in the dark and illuminating haggard faces. The wind rattled in the stovepipe, but the fire still burned in the hearth.

The great bear, sensing its end at the hands of her own son, lay down and waited for the arrow to pierce her heart. Arcas steadied his breath to calm his beating heart. Two hearts beating in tandem. Zeus, who had been watching this, intervened, just as Arcas was about to release the arrow, and transformed him into a little bear so that he would know his mother once more. Great bear and little bear both, were then sent to the heavens to reside together forever. Lonely no more, they sit side by side, mother and son...

The old man had stopped speaking and for a moment the men around the room thought he might be crying. The old man cleared his throat and stood up and walked to the hearth. He poked at the fire with a piece of kindling and sat back down against the wall. After a while, they could hear him snoring, his chest rising and falling in the dark.

The fire had long been dead by the time they were all awake in the morning, but the old man had got it going again with some broken planks he'd prised from the store cupboard wall. He now brewed coffee in a pan he'd taken from his satchel. He passed the pan round the room and each man poured some into their tin cup, dented and scratched from years of use. In their exhaustion of the night before, they'd not noticed on the scullery wall, a brace of heads, elk, stared back at them, mounted and hung, one above the other, listless and bored. *Perhaps a hunters cabin*, they thought.

They set off soon after they had finished the last of the coffee. The old man washed the pot with a handful of snow and put it back in his satchel. The snow had stopped falling sometime in the night, but it was hard-going trudging through what remained.

Two miles from the cabin they came across a body facedown in the snow. There were patches of blood about the corpse and they noticed that it was missing an arm. They buried the corpse in a shallow grave – the ground too frozen to bury it deeper. Some of the men said words over the grave and crossed themselves. They carried on their way, eager to reach the coast by sundown. Tomorrow they will be at sea. On they marched, and none looked back until the stranger's shallow grave was out of sight.

Acknowledgements

Meet the Fantastic Writers

Bob Bootman

I'd like to thank my family and friends, who are 'forced' to read my stuff, especially my wife, Gael, who has had to put up with me for many years and, has encouraged and supported me since I've been writing.

I'd also like to thank my friends in our writing group for their support, kindness and motivation and the inspirational Kelly, from Creative Hats, who has worked tirelessly to help us all improve over the last year.

Lewis Green

Lewis was born in Hitchin and grew up in Hertfordshire. He also lived in Yorkshire and Manchester before moving back down south and settling in Letchworth Garden City. By day he teaches small children how to use capital letters, finger spaces and full stops.

In his spare time, he himself uses capital letters, finger spaces and full stops, mostly in the correct place.

Lewis would like to thank everybody he has met during the creative writing courses he has attended for their kind words of encouragement, humour and motivation. He would also especially like to thank Kelly for keeping him motivated throughout and giving him the belief that being a 'writer' is indeed something that could be possible.

Martyn Kempson

Sixty years ago, or thereabouts Andy Eldred, a writer friend, and I got together to produce a poetry magazine featuring our poems. It was duplicated with a hand-coloured cover and a short run of perhaps 100 copies.

We called it after the name of the first cinema to come to Luton-The Anglo- American Electric Picture Palace.

Our marketing strategy was feeble and consisted mainly of standing by the entrance to Luton Railway Station at 8am trying to interest commuters rushing by with heads down as they tried to catch their trains. I think we sold three copies in a week and then gave up!

So here I am again at 74 trying to interest the public at large in my poetry ramblings alongside the fine efforts of my writer colleagues in this book. Some poets never give up.

After careers in education management, public libraries, an adviser to a charity, outdoor advertising, business development for a football club and exporting drums I am now safely retired and happy in Letchworth but still scribbling away in my notebook.

Nicola Warner

Nicola grew up in Hitchin, Hertfordshire. As a child she loved music, dancing and creating stories. Today she lives in her hometown with her husband, their two children, and their dog. In her spare time, she likes to make jewellery with gemstones, binge Netflix and read. She officially began writing in 2020, after joining a writing course at North Hertfordshire College. There she developed the confidence to finally put her ideas to paper.

She continued further writing courses with Creative Hats where she collaborated with a group of talented writers to publish: Fantastic Writers and Where to Find Them by Fantastic Writers in 2022. Nicola is currently working on finalising her first Novel to be published later in 2022.

Acknowledgements

If it wasn't for my loving husband, Martin, quite literally shoving me out of the door to attend a course I wouldn't be writing this now, never mind some of the contents in this book. So thank you dear husband, thank you for that gentle shove, thank you for reading the many drafts of work I have stuck under your nose and for always answering "Yes, very good" whenever I asked if it was ok.

Special thanks to my Mum, who didn't quite make editor (sorry mother) and my sister, Kylie, who always asked for the next installments, my close friends, Sabrina, Lakesha and Sarah, for taking the time to read anything I sent them.

Finally, I'd like to thank Kelly at Creative Hats, for the encouragement you have given me. You have been an amazing support throughout my writing journey. Fantastic Writers would never have existed without you.

Speaking of Fantastic Writers, you guys are all ... well ... Fantastic!

Paul Clark

My writing goes back more than fifty years. Apparently, I wrote loads of stories, I was never much good at drawing.

Writing came into my life again at university where the results were a collection of poems, mainly dark, which seemed to help my younger self finding his way in the world.

I made the mistake, with hindsight, of getting a friend on an English degree look then over. I don't recall her comments or feedback and I am not sure whether the poems still exist.

Study and work in various guises got in the way for the next thirty years. One evening at Stevenage campus I happened to read the room booking slip identified its course to be Creative Writing. Things changed!

I met a great teacher and a varied mix of good writers, although we didn't realize this at the time. It seems there was an expectation that as a teacher at the college I was a plant!

Through formal sessions and collaborative efforts, I feel I can now write pieces of various genre and the most exciting element is that an idea, picture, article, or piece of music can powerfully prompt a piece of prose or a chapter of my various writing projects. Writing has given me a new lease of life and hopefully a potential to make financial gains and recognition.

Tina Cooper

Who'd have thought I would ever be asked to write my bio? Not me, that's for darn sure. But asked I have been.

This splendid book came about because my classmates did most of the work. The weeks when all the planning and organizing were being planned and organized I was either staying away because of covid or at Harry Potter World.

Have you been to Harry Potter World? If not then you must go immediately. It doesn't matter whether or not you are a fan, you will be by the time you leave. All you need is to sell a body part or two on the black market and off you go.

We took our girls, my friend Mer and I. The girls were ten at the time so were very animated throughout but still, they didn't come even remotely close to how beside ourselves we adults were. I thought I might burst and we were still in the queue outside.

We didn't queue for long and were soon inside picking up our electronic tour guides that we never used. The adults ended up with two around their necks as the girls were bored with them pretty quickly. I'd also bought four guide books. Why did I do that? One per family would have sufficed but, you might remember my saying, I was beside myself.

We entered the main entrance area and were greeted by an enormous dragon hanging from the ceiling. Beyond this fabulous beastie were the restaurants and the butter beer but they would have to wait as we were being ushered into the main attraction.

Oh, I was asked to write three hundred words, boy can you use those up quickly if you're not looking!

Right then, best get on.

I was born in the …

Acknowledgment

I would like to take this opportunity to thank my fan for their unwavering support and endless supply of notebooks that I'll never write in because they are too lovely.

As my fan put it "oh my god, there's 31 books just on this shelf!"

Thank you to The Husband, my mum, Squidge and Boom for believing I could string a sentence together despite the fact that my mind wanders oh look there's a squirrel.

Tricia Ramsay

I was born in the East end of London called Stepney, which is now part of Towner Hamlets. The last in the family, who was born a 'cockney', to the sound of Bow bells. But was actually brought up in West London.

Orphaned by the age of eleven. My mother was a Londoner and my father a Yorkshire man. So, stubbornness, pride and resilience were already part of my DNA.

Even though I've lived outside of London for over

sixteen years. I find myself writing about it in my work. You know what they say 'you can take the girl out of London, but you can never take London, out of the girl'.

Creative Hats

www.creativehats.co.uk

Printed in Great Britain
by Amazon